ICED

A Resort to Murder Mystery

I0553818

Avery Daniels

**Blazing Sword
Publishing Ltd.**

Colorado Springs, CO

Avery Daniels/Blazing Sword Publishing, Ltd.
Colorado Springs, CO 80907
www.blazingswordpub.com

Publisher's Note: This is a work of fiction. Names, characters, places, and incidents are products of the author's imagination or are used fictitiously. Locales and public names are sometimes used for atmospheric purposes. Any resemblance to actual people, living or dead, is entirely coincidental.

Book Layout & Design ©2013-BookDesignTemplates.com

© Cover Art, Layout, and Design by Custom Covers

ICED/ Avery Daniels. -- 1st ed.
ISBN 978-0-9990318-0-3

Dedicated to all the people in my life who make this journey a little easier: friends who support and listen through good and tough times and fellow writers who plot with me and nurture my writing. I couldn't do this without each and every one of you.

.

Life being what it is, one dreams of revenge.

–Paul Gauguin

Chapter One

Today everything in my life changed.

I'm the events coordinator and membership manager, in training that is, at a five-star resort in Colorado. Some days, like today, it feels like I was sacrificed to some sadistic little idol somewhere. Coordination of conferences and meetings of all sizes in the resort's convention center facility was part of my training. But this particular event, a Leadership Luncheon that brought together the town's community leaders to network, was a challenge from the first minutes this morning.

"Julienne, this event must be executed with precision and perfection." Those are the favorite words of my boss, Chad. This particular event is a daylong exercise in patience.

Every job has its great parts and it's not so great. Today encompassed one of the more unpleasant aspects of my job. Occasionally, okay usually, the hardest part of my job is the customer relations and today was particularly difficult.   Some customers just can't be satisfied and some events are riddled with issues.

We were only serving a modest seventy-five attendees, but I had already been assailed with special requests and numerous complaints. Picky doesn't begin to cover it.

"How hard would it be to setup for a video presentation with a large screen and surround sound?"

"There are windows. It's too distracting, people will be watching the hotel guests walking around."

"Can we change the setup of room C from an L configuration to a U shape?   But only for that one session, then move it back."

"Can we get the Lobster for the buffet flown in that morning?   Scallops are out....Can we have the scallops after all?"

"Music piped in during the breaks?"

"No music piped in at all."

"Red tablecloths with white napkins."

"Royal blue tablecloths with white napkins."

"White tablecloths with yellow napkins."

"Candles on mirrors for lunch centerpieces."

"Fresh flowers for centerpieces."

The changes continued even after the event started.

The Convention Center, with its classic European décor, had a small lobby area with a few potted trees and plants on column stands. The rest extended down a hallway with two large areas on each side that could be divided into smaller rooms via partitions that extend from the walls as needed. The space could be up to eight small rooms, four on each side, or any combination from one to four rooms per side of the hallway.

The hallway was wide with several half-circle console tables including marble tops holding large dried floral arrangements and a few elegant chairs. The walls displayed large paintings of the Italian countryside and vineyards with carved gold gilt frames.

I was in a partitioned room overseeing the set up of the lunch buffet. The Italian Renaissance architecture was accentuated with interior details and décor that created a European elegance, all lit with the warm glow of a massive amber glass chandelier.

The room was a rectangle with the entrance from the hallway to one end and the door to the catering staging area at the opposite end. The buffet table was along the wall next to the staging door so wait staff could easy restock food items. The six-person round tables covered in rich golden linens were scattered strategically throughout the room to allow easy traffic flow. The thick carpet felt plush and cloud-like under foot.

I was surveying the buffet table with a critical eye. The five-foot long ice sculpture of a swordfish occupied the center of the table and looked as though it was caught in mid leap, frolicking in a wave and ready to dive back into an unseen ocean. My stomach growled, as the succulent smells of seafood teased my nose. The attendees would be returning to this room for their lunch and keynote speaker shortly.

"Brad, where are the crab leg metal crackers and little forks? Can you grab a few dozen and bring them right away?" Brad, slim and serious, had joined the team only two months ago and was picking up extra hours at every opportunity. He had asked to work this event as soon as I blocked out the time on the schedule. This would give him a good paycheck. He was lanky and took off with an easy loping stride to the staging area through the back door.

The door to the staging area had barely closed when I felt a hand grab hold of my derriere with an iron hard grip.

"This is more like it honey. I haven't had any fun today."

I whirled around and stumbled back. "Don't touch the staff. That includes me, Pastor Tom." I practically shouted. Pastor Tom Drake was well known around town, and getting national attention lately with his mega church. He was included in the luncheon due to his influence, but he was just Pastor Tom to me since he was a local guy who started his church and radio ministry from his garage.

I had contended with bad behavior before, but never this grabby. I think I was going to have a bruise left from his vicious hand.

"You're not being very fri...friendly." I noticed his eyes were droopy and then I caught a whiff of the scotch he must have gotten at the Gilded Hornet pub next to the convention center building.

I decided to alert security we needed a person to monitor the rest of the event and turned to go. His iron hand grabbed hold of my arm and yanked me to him. Without a thought, I took my knee to his groin and enjoyed watching his mouth form an "O" as his breath whooshed out. I broke free and backed away. I wasn't turning my back on him again.

"I will see you fired for that you bitch." He whispered with a jagged voice.

He couldn't do that, at least I was pretty sure he couldn't. I guess I'd find out. I rubbed my still smarting arm where he grabbed it. Brad would be back or the event participants would start to wander in so he couldn't do much more, but I didn't want to stay and find out. I backed out the door to the hallway toward the lobby and took my cell phone from my pants pocket.

"Hey Ron, we have a person under the influence at the luncheon in Convention Center. Can you spare someone for the afternoon?"

"I'll make sure somebody's there immediately Julienne. How bad is this guy?"

"Well, I'll probably have a black-and-blue handprint on my arm and ...my backside." I took a deep breath.

"Son of a ... I'll be right there. You stay away from him." *Like I would go near that Neanderthal again, pastor or not.*

The other participants were starting to exit the smaller break out session rooms and meander to the banquet room and bathrooms. The noise level began to creep upward from multiple conversations competing to be heard.

There was a loud crash of metal from the banquet room and a participant jerked open the door and froze in place. "Oh sh..." The participant's mouth gaped and his eyes were large circles.

I ran over to the open door and saw Pastor Tom impaled through the chest with the sharp end of the Swordfish ice sculpture, from his back right through to the front. His head was forward against his chest. Blood, running down the swordfish tip that jutted from his chest, dripping to the carpet. Drip, drip, drip in a macabre but surreal scene.

"Crap, this isn't good," was my first thought, followed closely by "how did that swordfish kill him?" I wasn't going with the obvious answer of God's judgment.

I looked up to the back door to the staging room at Anete Kruze, one of the servers. The catering facilities were in the hotel, so the food was brought across to the Convention Center and staged in the room back there. Anete was holding an empty metal pan usually filled with silverware that she had dropped on the floor and were now scattered around her. She was frozen in place and trembling.

I had been trained in basic first aid and CPR, but Pastor Tom was clearly past that point. I turned and yelled above the gathering din of voices, "Somebody call 911. Is there a Doctor present?" I was relieved I didn't start screaming or faint at the blood, if I could just stay focused on what I needed to do I could maintain my professional demeanor.

Nobody stepped forward. A few had grabbed their smart phones. Oh no, this would be all over Twitter and Facebook. As everybody filed into the wide hallway, the buzz of hushed conversations began around me.

"Is it...?"

"It's Pastor Drake."

"No, it can't be Drake, who would kill him?"

"Did you get a photo?"

"Everyone, please put your phones away now. No photos or video please." I kept my voice commanding without croaking like a frog.

Then the crowd hushed and parted for a woman, looking around confused. She leaned forward just enough to look inside and began to quake.

"No. Tom... It can't be him, no." She turned and scanned the crowd and began calling out, "Tom, where are you?"

My sluggish mind realized she must be Pastor Tom's wife...or widow, when a man pushed through the crowd and led her away talking gently to her. My heart clenched as I hurt for her.

The crowd parted once again for Ron, our head of Security, as he rushed over.

"What's going on?" But he quickly saw the body impaled on the ice sculpture, walked over and gradually reached his hand out to Pastor Tom's neck for a pulse. After rubbing his eyes and a few deep breaths, he commanded the gathering staff at the back staging door to leave the room and not to enter until he had a chance to talk with each of them.

"Julienne, nobody comes in this room but the police. Do you hear me?" I nodded. What should I do though? I looked at all the food spread out on the table and realized the voices behind me were grumbling.

"Everyone, lunch will be served in the break out rooms you had your sessions in. Please return to those rooms and the wait staff will be serving soon." I didn't have a clue what we would serve since the buffet was out of the question.

The rest was a blur as I attempted to get the attendees fed sandwiches and salad and direct the emergency personnel with a stretcher, who wouldn't disturb the crime scene by even entering the room until the forensic people were done. When the forensic techs arrived, they weren't happy.

"Ice! Are you kidding me? The weapon and any fingerprints are melting before we even get set up."

I fielded calls from Chad who couldn't get away from an important meeting and then assisted the stone-faced police.

I started as the hotel's front desk associate and worked my way up. It's my dream to manage large resorts around the world and I'm fortunate to have the on-the-job manager training position at a five-star resort in my hometown. But this...situation... hadn't been covered in any of my training to date, so I was going on instinct and hoping I didn't mess it up.

I was one of the first questioned, but by that time I was so frazzled I kept the image of a huge Mojito fixed in my mind to keep me going.

"Ms. LaMere, we appreciate your keeping all the participants here and calm. What exactly was this, a conference?"

I got the sourest faced uniformed officer of the group, not that any of them looked likely to show a comforting smile, but this man's eyes said "You are all criminals and I'm watching you."

"It was a networking event for influential people in the community. I don't know any more details, but I can point out the organizer of the event for you." I had been standing for hours and my practical low-heeled shoes were nonetheless pinching my swollen feet and I was hitting the exhaustion wall.

"I understand from your security manager that you had called him about a drunk accosting you. We'll need to speak to that person especially. Who was it?"

"It was..." It had just occurred to me how this might look. I just nodded my head towards the banquet room. Sourpuss's eyebrow lifted while his eyes narrowed.

"How did the..." he checked his notes, "ice sculpture spear him through?" Voice monotone and cold.

"How would I know? I wasn't in the room." I took a slow breath. I was a victim here too. Sure, I was still alive, but I had been assaulted by the right reverend. I felt like I was about to become Pastor Tom's victim again even in his death.

"You didn't put up a fight and somehow spear him?"

I decided to just rip the Band-Aid off fast. "I kneed him in the crotch as hard as I could and left to call security. The smaller sessions were disbanding when we all heard a loud crash. It was only then that ... that...that we saw him like that." I waved my hand to indicate Pastor Tom's direction. I was reliving it in my mind and shivered. That Mojito may not quiet my increasingly churning stomach or my developing headache.

"When you last saw him, how was he?"

"Doubled over holding his crotch and trying to breathe." I normally would have gotten a smidgen of satisfaction from that, but not now. I had to fight to not fidget.

"Did he say anything?"

"Well he ... said he would have me fired for that." It was out of my mouth before my mind could clamp my flapping lips shut. I should have lied, I was screaming to myself. I know I didn't kill him, but it sure sounded bad the more I talked.

"Didn't that make you mad?"

"I wish I could tell you that he was the worst example of abuse I have had to endure, but sadly he's not. Trust me, some folks aren't nice people at all. I wasn't mad nor did I kill him, if that's where you're headed."

He made some notes and didn't seem impressed by my passionate speech. "How long was it from when you left the victim and heard the 'loud crash'?"

"I would say three to five minutes, no more." *Oh crap, oh crap.* That looks even worse for me. I clamped my mouth shut. Tight.

"Anything else you can think of?"

"I think he was drunk. He smelled like booze."

The press arrived and my sour policeman jumped into action to keep the news cameras and reporters at a distance. Detective Lawrence then questioned me. He asked me several of the same questions, plus many more. He had such a stern look and serious expression that I swear a smile would split his face from hairline to chin. I knew from the cop shows the repeated questions were a tactic to get my story tripped up if I was lying. I didn't like the feel of being grilled as though I was the killer.

Chapter Two

Chad finally showed up and had taken control, giving orders all around. It was late in the afternoon before I was free to leave. My feet wanted a soak and I wanted to banish from my mind the feel of Pastor Drake grabbing me, and the image of his body impaled. I wanted to forget that vacant stare from his lifeless eyes, and I really wanted to quit feeling like I would have handcuffs slapped on me any moment.

I had just left the convention center and started walking away from the complex of buildings including the resort and my office towards home. I didn't want to walk home, even though it was only five minutes away. A car pulled up next to me.

"Um, Miss LaMere. Can I give you a lift home? After all this, you shouldn't be walking alone. Besides, I think you won't get far." He nodded his head towards the reporters on the other side of the road, kept at a distance by the police. Ah, the speed of social media sharing and cell phones. I hadn't considered news crews following me, hounding me for details I didn't want to ever think of again until the sight of the sensationalist news gauntlet.

I typically kept my private life, including where I live, to myself at work. I didn't like mixing work with my private life since I was training in management, but I really didn't want reporters descending on my home sanctuary. I sighed. These were extenuating circumstances and everyone knew I lived close since I walked.

"I appreciate it, Brad. Please keep it to yourself where I live, though."

"Oh, no problem." We were quiet except for directions. As soon as the car turned off the main road and into the townhome complex with nicely landscaped grounds, I saw a small crowd loitering in front of my particular home. *Great, I now had to run a different sort of gauntlet...my inquiring neighbors.*

They no doubt had heard the emergency vehicle sirens and seen any TV news and were awaiting my arrival. I live in a unique townhome complex with a collection of colorful neighbors. Brad pulled over at the curb outside my stucco two-story townhome unit. I felt like I was in high school again and my peers were sizing me up on the first day of school after break. Brad was slowly inching the car away, looking at my house more intently than any realtor. *So much for my separating work and private life.* Probably wasn't a good idea after all.

Delores and Beverly approached me. I was about to be grilled by the masters of interrogation. The police had nothing on these two. Bright copper haired Beverly was turning seventy next year, but the short tattooed dynamo rarely sat still for long. Delores was about five years younger, was taller, and had a penchant for wine, lots of it.

"Let's start with the good news. Have you seen the hot new guy that moved into number eighty-two?" Beverly set her perfectly plucked eyebrows dancing up and down. I hadn't seen that one coming. I had fully expected to be hounded about Drake's murder.

I glanced across the street and noticed a small rental van and one guy unloading that I'd missed until now. Hey, I was still shaken up. He was broad shouldered with rippling muscles showing under his short-sleeved rust t-shirt, shoulder length wavy dark brown hair, and long legs.

But, even as pleasantly distracting as he was, I just couldn't give the "hot new guy" any serious thought at the moment. I felt a little nauseous as visions of Pastor Tom's dead body hanging like a limp scarecrow on the end of the icy swordfish nose with dripping blood continued to pop into my mind.

"Beverly, I've had a bad day. I want to soak in a hot bath with a cold drink and forget what has happened."

"So, we'll meet you in the club house hot tub with a pitcher of margaritas ready." Delores patted her short hair. "Maybe number eighty-two can join us to relax his muscles."

"Nope, I'm not letting you guys get me drunk again. I can't keep up with you two."

"Light weight." Beverly shot at me.

"Then you'll have to tell us now what happened to Pastor Drake." Delores chimed in.

I made my polite apologies and sprinted up my front steps. To top off my day, I was out of mint for the Mojitos. I had to resort to a glass of white wine for my steaming bubble bath.

Chapter Three

Behind the hotel was a man-made lake that was more a sprawling pond with ducks and paddleboats for guests. I retreated to the lake often, its soothing glassy surface lined with trees lining its edge was a calming salve. The slightly chilled morning air combined with the colors of the changing trees invigorated me, renewed my focus. Autumn was my favorite season. The blazing vivid colors painted the world bright and bold. It was contrary to my dark thoughts. I doubt if I got more than an hour of sleep, so I opted to go into work early but the beauty of the lake beckoned.

I didn't have experience dealing with dead bodies or death in general, except for my mother's passing when I was twelve. I didn't view my mother's body at the funeral; I didn't want that to be my last memory of her. Perhaps that's why I'm so haunted by the lifeless stare I saw yesterday. I couldn't help feel everything in my world had changed in that instant.

I was on my second circuit around the lake when I met Anete Kruze walking towards me, lost in her own thoughts.

"Anete, how're you doing after yesterday?" She was the unfortunate server who walked in to find a Pastor Tom skewered on the ice swordfish.

"Oh, I did not see you, ma'am. I'm not due into work for a few minutes." She looked at her watch, then glanced around while her hands fidgeted with her coat zipper.

"I understand. I needed to get outside a little too." I said. She was pale and her eyes were blood shot.

I wanted to ask her if she saw anybody else in the room when she found the body but told myself the police would have covered that.

"Anete, if you need to talk to somebody about yesterday, the company can get you a few counseling sessions. You don't have to face it alone."

"I will be okay ma'am. I'll be right as rain, don't worry." Her brow crinkled.

"Well, just know that if you have a hard time from what you saw, it's natural. There's no shame in talking to somebody. Claudia can get you set up."

Rather than dwell on it, I planned on delving headfirst into work. But, I'd like to help Anete. I made a mental note to myself to see if we could bring in some counselors one day for any employees to consult. Anete scurried away, no doubt afraid to be late for her shift serving breakfast.

My office was located in the main hotel of the Colorado Springs Hotel and Resort complex of buildings. The entire property took several acres of land and was originally built in 1918. The hotel and restaurants with its impressive entry drive and man-made lake behind it were built first, then across the street from the hotel entry the pub and convention center with several shop spaces such as dry cleaners or flower shop were built. More specialty shops adjacent to the hotel were added like jewelry, art gallery, high-end clothing, golf pro shop, theater and playhouse, then to the south the championship golf courts stretch to the east, tennis courts, fitness center, and spa complex remain close to the hotel.

More luxury accommodations were built on the other side of the lake with a grand ballroom, then plush and private cottages were built on open space next to the tennis courts. It was a sprawling complex catering to every need with walkways, lush gardens, and landscaping throughout. But, my idyllic Shangri-La had been forever tainted with the violent spilling of blood.

The Pastor Drake's stabbing had taken place in the convention center, which was across the street from the hotel. I headed back to my office, grateful I wouldn't have to see the convention center if I entered the hotel from the lake-side back entrance.

I was in my closet-sized office with its metal desk and laminate wood surface and two mismatched chairs, one for me and one for a visitor. Manager-in-training wasn't glamorous. My desk surface had tidy stacks of work in progress, and my few decorating touches were reserved for framed posters of world famous resorts. I was wearing my usual blazer and slacks with a coordinating blouse, button earrings, and fine gold chain necklace.

I left my door open, needing to feel closer to the rest of the employees and normal flurry of activity. I needed to feel connected to the living rather than cut off with the door closed.

This also meant I could hear every bit of complaint or gossip, which was why I tended to close my door. Today the staff had plenty to talk about as they gathered in the hallway a few feet down from my office. Employee voices drifted to me.

"I heard that Pastor Tom was no saint. He preached about family and marriage but he didn't practice it." Tamara stated in her twangy voice.

A self-assured male voice I recognized from the hotel maintenance staff chimed in. "Everybody says that about a pastor, especially one so outspoken and political. You can't believe everything you hear."

"I know somebody who was told by a girl at Tom's church how he showed too much interest in the teen girls then lost interest after a while. Cold hearted, like. It's the truth. I bet that's what got him killed"

"I still say you can't believe such talk. It's more likely he was killed because he was so outspoken about moral issues and our godless government." I could just envision maintenance guy's wide stance with arms crossed.

"Maybe elsewhere, but not here with more church organizations and Christian businesses per capita, except maybe Salt Lake City." Tamara countered.

They continued to banter back and forth, but I had tuned them out already. A thought had occurred to me. Would the fact that Pastor Tom died at one of our events damage our business, our bookings? I had been focused on the police eyeing me as the killer, but what about the hotel? Would it affect the reputation of the Colorado Springs Hotel and Resort long term?

The phone rang as I contemplated the ramifications. I answered to a strong male voice.

"I need to cancel an event. I will be moving my Christmas event elsewhere." The insistent tone didn't allow for any discussion.

I looked up the details on the event and found it was for two hundred people.

"May I ask if you've found another venue for your event yet?"

"Not that it's any of your business, but I haven't begun calling."

"I can finalize your cancellation, but once I do that I will be calling the organizations on my waiting list. The holiday season is usually booked far ahead of time." I looked through the notes on this event. "I see you booked this back in January for this Christmas. Most venues of this size will be booked up already."

I let that soak in for a bit. This really wasn't the time to cancel without a solid backup plan. I was put on hold and after several minutes pacing and waiting the person returned.

"We'll think of something." The voice wasn't as insistent or sure this time though. I just might have persuaded him.

"Tell you what. Why don't I give you twenty-four hours before I process your cancellation and open this date up for people on the waiting list? If you find an available place, the cancellation will go through. But, if you change your mind and call me back before this time tomorrow."

"Well...I'll get back to you." I may have saved that booking. As soon as I hung up, the phone rang again. I repeated the process three more times – pacing included, potentially saving all but the one. I even offered ten percent off to the hold-out, feeling it was better to lose a little money rather than lose a good client.

If I had doubted the impact of Pastor Tom's death to the resort, I was positive now. I was about to get some on-the-job training because we needed some damage control. I could put my mind on this and not the death or my fears of being an easy scapegoat. Besides, this was part of my training, although I never expected this situation.

I talked with Chad and we spent a few hours devising some promotional campaigns to offset the potential lost business. I stopped pacing and felt better doing something constructive.

Then Claudia and Chad included me as they developed a press statement expressing the hotel's deep regrets to Pastor Tom's family and congregation of several thousand for their loss to be read at the press conference we scheduled to take place in a few hours. I took the opportunity to discuss with Claudia getting some counselors to come in and talk to the employees who worked the disastrous luncheon. Within the next few days, she hoped to have counselors setup to talk with employees in a spare office at the hotel.

I hadn't eaten anything all day when we gathered for the press conference in a side room in one of the resort's fine dining restaurants.   Smells of Beef Burgundy, polished wood, and a salacious story at hand mingled as several reporters with microphones and two cameramen filed in.

Low murmurs filtered to us at the podium mixed with clatters and clinks from the kitchen and the occasional maître d's subdued instructions to wait staff as they prepared for the dinner crowd.

Normally, we would have held it in the convention center, but I contended the reporters would be busy trying to take pictures of the crime scene that still had yellow police tape cordoning off the room.

Claudia stood at the podium we had setup. She read from our statement, just like we had practiced. I looked out at the twelve reporters, surprised to see the major networks represented and the New York Times alongside our local news from Colorado Springs and of course Denver. The shining star of Pastor Tom had drawn a national audience with his book and radio show and likewise his death now drew the press.

My gaze screeched to a halt at a woman with dishwater blond hair, brown eyes, and average height that seemed familiar to me. She looked my way and a sneer appeared on her face. *Who the heck was she and why did she seem familiar?*

We decided not to take questions, so when Claudia finished and thanked everyone for their attendance, the three of us escaped out a back employee door and met in Claudia's office for chocolate rewards.

By the end of the day we had a few more cancelled events. But, I had developed autumn promotions to be placed in the local newspaper and some golf and vacation magazines as last minute additions before they went to press.

By the time I quit for the day I had stopped obsessing on the dead body. I was walking home to Resort Shadows townhomes, enjoying the mild warmth with a promise of approaching crisp autumn in the air. It occurred to me that it didn't take long for the world to rush headlong onward. Soon Pastor Tom Drake's tragic death would be forgotten.

I had just reached the stairs to my townhome with keys in hand when I heard my name called. I turned to identify who had called me, hoping this wouldn't take long.

When I turned I discovered my new neighbor walking towards me. He was about six inches taller than me. Now that I got a good look, I could see why Delores and Beverly were in a flutter, even at their ages.

He may not be a fireman like Delores drools over, but he was handsome, with shoulder length wavy hair that gave him a disreputable and dangerous aura, big hazel eyes with long lashes, a defined jaw that suggested inner strength more than stubbornness, broad shoulders, and muscular arms shown to perfection with a navy blue t-shirt and dark blue snug jeans. No sagging or faded jeans for this one. I was positive he'd find himself plenty of attention from the female residents of the Resort Shadows community. I had to keep from melting under the intense look he leveled at me that compelled me to tell him every fantasy I ever had. I mentally slapped myself.

"I was hoping you could help me." He drew closer and lowered his voice. "Please don't direct me to Delores either." His lopsided smile was infectious. "She's a dear, but I think she's trying to set me up with her daughter."

I chuckled, "Oh, I would hate to deprive her of a chance to get to know you better. How'd you know my name?"

"I've been repeatedly pointed in your direction by Beverly. Please rescue me from the kind attention

Delores insists on lavishing on me. If you reject me, you'll prove a heartless neighbor. I can't take anymore pies or cookies and offers to meet her daughter." He was close enough for me to smell his cologne, a warm and spicy scent. *Steady, focus.*

"What can I help you with?" I realized I was smiling in response to his grin.

"How serious are the pet restrictions here?"

I had to think for a bit, get past his eyes, hair, and muscles. "No more than one large pet per dwelling I believe." But, he likely already knew that. "I don't think birds or fish count. I don't know of a case where it has been challenged so I can't really tell you."

He leaned closer. "That isn't too bad. I can bring Roulette, my sheltie, home from my parents then." *Seriously? Who names their pet Roulette?*

"So what is it you do for a living Mr....?"

"Mason Sheridan." He captured my hand and placed a lingering kiss on it while those hazel eyes never broke from looking into mine. I had never had my hand kissed before, let alone looked at so intensely. I wasn't sure what to do. I felt heat rising in my cheeks and breathing was taking thought. My heart was pounding.

I became aware of my appearance. I wished I was dressed a bit more feminine than the champagne pink cashmere blouse, merlot colored raw silk side slit skirt and matching pearl necklace and earrings I had worn for work.

"I'm a photographer and sometimes..." still holding my hand he moved to whisper in my ear with that velvet voice, "I play high stakes poker." He stepped back but still held my hand captive. *Well, that explained the name of his dog.*

I bet the entire community would be talking about our intimate little meeting in the open. I could feel the eyes behind curtains watching us.

I took possession of my hand again, for it would have stayed there all night left up to itself. "What kind of photography?" I didn't know what to make of the poker confession, so I was staying with the safer topic.

"Wildlife, scenery, underwater, some models, and catalog work. You may have seen my work in several calendars or a few coffee table books."

I was at a loss for what to say. He photographed wild animals and models plus played poker. Somehow that just seemed like a television series that would be on the men's cable network so every man could live vicariously through him. I bet he dated models in-between hands of poker. How very Bond-like.

"Well Mr. Mason Sheridan it's a pleasure to meet you, but I've had a long day at work and must be going. I trust you and your Sheltie Roulette will enjoy Resort Shadows."

I had switched to my resort professional persona. I wasn't in the market anyway. Brandon was my guy. I'd known Brandon since high school. Since he was my cousin Loring's best friend, he was practically a member of the family. We've dated the last year or so. It's very casual and I never asked for more. It's been enough for me. Brandon had even offered to take me out tonight but I had convinced him I wasn't up to it.

Bond Jr. looked disappointed. "Of course. Beverly and Delores said something about a death at the resort while you were working. That must be very stressful." He bowed his head ever so slightly and then winked at me. He turned and walked back across the street to his townhome whistling. I could swear he was whistling the Bond theme "Nobody Does It Better."

I'm more a Jason Bourne girl anyway. Truly.

I didn't have much of an appetite so I lost myself playing music on my clarinet for the evening. I immersed myself in a few classical pieces and then turned to smoky sensuous blues. Maybe I would watch a Bourne movie with some Mojitos. I had gotten mint.

Chapter Four

I went to work the next morning expecting to be back to normal, business as usual. Maybe not fully, but close. I knew there would likely be a few more cancellation of events, but I was cautiously optimistic it would be slowing. I dressed with care as if that would make a difference how the day would go. I wore teal slacks with a matching lightweight suede blazer, dove gray blouse, quarter inch wide gold snake chain necklace, and button gold earrings.

I placed the key into my office door lock, thinking only of the day ahead. When a voice, seemingly right next to my ear, boomed.

"Ms. LaMere, I need a few minutes of your time."

I jumped, not out of my skin but darn close. With hand to heart and my blood racing, I gradually turned. The same slow turn the heroine does in a horror movie, knowing what is behind her will be the death of her. I felt that same horror as I faced Detective Lawrence.

He was just outside Chad's office, feet apart and arms crossed. Chad peeked out of his office, saw me, and shut his door with a whoosh. I felt more alone in that moment than when my Mom died, at least I had my dad and family around me then.

I cleared my throat. "Why?" My voice came out anemic. I straightened my back and took a breath. *Don't let him see your fear.* Or was that with growling dogs? Oh well, same thing really.

"I want you to walk me through what happened." No crumbled overcoat here, he wore a modest suit, no tie, and scuffed shoes. His face was average but there was the sense that he didn't smile often. I guess if I had his job I might not smile much either.

"But, I did. I gave two or three statements day-before-yesterday explaining it." I hoped my voice was stronger and I tried to keep any whine from mingling with my fear.

"Yes, I'm fully aware of that. I want you to demonstrate your movements. Now." He motioned with his arm out to proceed before him.

That cautious optimism from earlier had turned tail and disappeared. I felt singled out, and dread had settled into the pit of my stomach. I noticed employees we passed stared and whispered among themselves.

We returned to the same room – *the scene of the crime,* the buffet was still set up except those items that required refrigeration, which they had taken away. But, everything else was still in place, the plates, silverware, metal crab leg crackers, crab forks, serving utensils, glasses, napkins and so on. It felt different, tainted, or maybe stripped of joy as if the police presence had spoiled the usual energy, or perhaps it was the murder had slain the sense of safety. A chill went down my spine. *Somebody walked over my grave.*

At the edge of the buffet table was a large bloodstain on the luxurious carpet, now an angry rust brown declaration. Perhaps that was the source of the strange smell I couldn't quite place. My stomach clenched and I was grateful I hadn't eaten breakfast.

"I understand that you were the last person to see Pastor Drake alive," He droned. Was this a trick question?

"Except the murderer." I wasn't going to fall for that. I crossed my arms.

"You said to the police officer taking your statement that you had words with Pastor Drake. Care to tell me about that?" He had a great poker face. There was no indication just how I was to take this question.

"We didn't argue really, he forced himself on me, grabbed my butt and arm. I have bruises even. I kneed him real good and left to call Ron. Should we get photos of the bruises if this is a problem?" I was starting to get irritated. Better than having an anxiety attack, like I felt coming on at the sight of the dried blood.

"Really? An upstanding and nationally respected clergyman, a leader in this community and he is going to assault you when somebody could walk in at any moment? Really?" His face never changed, granite. His voice inflections oozed disbelief though.

"Yeah, really. Did you get his blood alcohol level back yet? Because he was a polluted leader of the community." I raised my eyebrows at him. *Touché.* I was not to blame here. I was a victim of assault from that lecherous leader.

"How long was it from the time you left Pastor Tom and the server found him?"

"As I explained already it was only a few minutes. I ran from the room into the lobby and called security on my cell phone immediately. I didn't want any scenes if his drunken state should cause more problems. Shortly after the phone call, the break-out sessions had dismissed and people were milling around. That's when the crash of falling silverware came through the doors." I thought I was calm and cool even though I felt I was the sole suspect. I shifted from one foot to the other.

"Let me summarize what you're telling me. You have a disagreement with the victim and you are the only witness to this alleged assault. You said he threatened to have you fired. In mere minutes from your leaving the room, he's found dead. In those short few minutes somebody approached him, shish kabobed him with the spear-end of the ice sculpture from the table and left without anybody noticing. Does that about sum it up?"

"I don't know anything after the point I left the room. But he was alive. Maybe doubled over in pain holding his nuts, but alive." *Oh no, no, no. Call me paranoid but I felt Detective Lawrence was looking forward to arresting me. Crap.*

"See, you're the only witness to this little altercation you claim to have had." He tapped his chin with his pen. "Maybe you like powerful men or just married men. Maybe he was turning you down and it got physical, he said he would report your behavior and things got out of hand, you tried to slap him or shove him – somehow you got rough and the table is struck causing the ice sculpture to dislodge. You shove him onto the sharp icy end. Or maybe it was an accident and he gets shoved. It's happened before." Spoken with a poker face. *Not so paranoid after all.*

"No, that's not what happened. There may not be a witness to the assault, but why would I say anything and leave myself wide open to exactly this sort of suspicion if I had killed him, even accidentally?" I gulped a breath of air. "If I were the killer, I'd have shut up and nobody would have known he assaulted me. I left him alive and have no reason to hide anything." Ha, take that. I was thinking clearly. *Keep breathing.* Inside I was panicking. This could not be happening. *Keep breathing.*

He asked a few more questions and then had me reenact my account of what happened. By the time I was dismissed to go back my job, my fists and jaws were clenched and a headache was fast approaching.

Back in my office, I sat like a lump in my chair staring at the framed posters of exotic resorts around the world. How could this be happening? I had worked hard to get into the resort management-training program. I had fought with my father over it. He finally relented figuring I would meet some country club guy and get married, which is what he wants for his little princess. My having a career was definitely not in his plan.

Oh no! Dad. I laid my head on my desk. He'll no doubt tell me how I should've listened to him and married a lawyer or doctor – but not gone into resort management. He was going lecture me, or worse.

But I didn't want to raise a family, at least not yet. I wanted to work resorts all over the world, Barbados, Hawaii, Paris, mountain resorts, beach resorts, ski resorts. I wanted to see a bit of the world first.

"Julienne, we need to talk." My head whipped up. Chad closed the door and sat down in the visitor chair. Could this day get any worse? Scratch that.

He wanted to know what the police had wanted. I gave him a detailed report, no executive summary this time.

"The Detective talked with me before you came in. He only asked questions about you, your work performance, your personal life. It didn't sound good." He studied me. My eye developed a nervous tick.

"Chad, they haven't charged me with anything, they haven't taken me to the station for questioning. They're just shaking some trees to see what falls out." *Yeah, that was it. Sure.* My eye kept twitching. "Now I have to check on those ads for the autumn promotion." Chad left without saying anything more, his eyes holding a stern look. The employees that passed in the hall looked in with quick glances and chattered with each other. I was the entertainment for the day apparently.

I got a few things done but the afternoon brought an onslaught of phone calls from my family about how they had been questioned by the Detective. Well, my aunt and uncle. Aunt Regina assured me she had not told my father.

"But he'll find out soon enough. Pastor Drake's death is making national news, so he'll be calling you soon I imagine. Just be strong."

"Oh, Aunt Regi, it doesn't look good. I seem to be the last person to see him before he was killed."

"They asked us about you and Brandon too, honey. Not sure why they would ask about your relationship, how could that matter?" She puzzled while my heart stopped.

I remembered Detective Lawrence's wild scenario where I made advances on Pastor Tom. It seemed the police were trying to prove that outrageous speculation.

Chapter Five

I didn't have much time to contemplate my predicament because shortly after hanging up from sweet aunt Regina, the phone rang.

"What in the blazes has been going on?" My meddling but well-meaning father. I raised my arms to beseech the heavens and mouthed *"What else can go wrong?"* Scratch that.

"I turn on the news to catch thirty seconds about a murder that just happens to occur where my only daughter works and nobody's told me. Explain yourself, Julienne." I could envision his stormy gray eyes flashing bolts of lightning. I jumped up and closed my office door. No need for other employees to hear me arguing with my dad. I sat back down.

"Daddy, I'm glad you called." I opted for the dear daughter approach. "Sorry I didn't call. I've been busy and exhausted from all this. I saw the body and I can't get it out of my head. I haven't slept well." Which was all true. I just didn't want the lecture. Why do dads think they have to lecture? I grabbed a paper clip to bend.

"Julie, you'd be sleeping fine if you'd settled down and were raising a family. This is what happens when you insist on a career before finding security and building a home."

"The sleeping with kids is debatable. If I recall listening to every new parent they get very little sleep with babies and teething or when the child gets older and has nightmares or gets sick. That argument won't work on me dad." That quickly the sweet daughter approach was out the window. The paper clip was straightened now.

"Why do you have to fight me on this? I want what is best for you and it sure as the dickens isn't stumbling over dead bodies."

"Dad, if you want what's best for me you'll want what makes me happy and that's my career. You made something of your life and I have your love of work and adventurous spirit. I'd think you would want to encourage me in this rather than fighting me." Two could play this game and I'd been preparing this speech for a while now.   The paper clip was wrapped around my little finger.

"Perhaps you're too much like me. I want you taken care of not working hard, but it appears you'll deny your aging father his final dream come true." Dad was on a roll, laying the guilt on thick. I rolled my eyes. "I want to give you away at your wedding. I want grand children, Julie." Finally, he had dropped the pretenses and the meat of the matter was now on the table, so to speak. I flicked the paper clip across the room.

"So that's it. Dad, unless you aren't telling me something about your health, there's time for me to get married. I'm not opposed to the idea you know, it's just the timing. I have nothing against having children... well maybe. But I don't want a life of regrets." There, I said it. I didn't want to marry just for the sake of marrying or have children just to give him grandchildren. When the time came, I'd know it and it would fall into place.

"Enough of that princess, tell me what happened to the pompous ass Pastor Drake and don't leave anything out." He listened to my entire tale and I began to think I should just record it and hit play the next time somebody asked. I included my disastrous talk with the detective and how it didn't look dire but neither did it look good.

"Should I contact a lawyer for you? I don't want to wait until it's too late, after all." He was in his element now, directing and taking charge. He'd retired from a senior management position in a Department of Defense contracting company three years ago, leaving me the townhome in hopes I would snag a rich husband there. He'd been a bit rudderless since he retired and decided to move to a warmer climate. So he now lived in sunny Florida and ran a small tourist company. I knew he just wanted to help.

"A lawyer's not a bad idea, maybe I wouldn't feel like a fish on a policeman's hook being reeled in. Dad, you know I didn't do anything to that jerk, right? I didn't encourage him or anything to provoke his grabbing me." My voice started to crack. I was a grown woman, but that encounter had shaken me nearly as much as seeing the dead vacant stare.

"Honey, the man is lucky somebody beat me to it. Of course, you didn't do anything to deserve that. I may be a bit old fashioned but there is never a reason to treat a woman like he did. Never. I don't care what the circumstances or situation." I brushed a tear from my cheek and took a breath.

"That man was a bully and needed to be kicked in the cojones. I'm proud of you for standing up for yourself, dear. Don't you forget it." I love my dad. Yeah, he can be overbearing and bull headed sometimes, but he never let me down.

"Thanks, dad, I needed that more than you will probably ever know." Wow, I was getting weepy. I wiped another line tear away. "So how is Juanita doing? You two still planning a vacation to the Virgin Islands together?"

Dad had not dated since Mom died, until I was living on my own. He had remained fit and had gained some distinguished gray on his temples, and was successful with good retirement funds. He was a catch. I suspected he was comparing every woman to my Mom's memory until he moved to Florida. He dated a few ladies and eventually met Juanita, a woman completely unlike my mother, and they had been dating for a solid six months now. Her family owned and ran a popular restaurant on Key West.

We chatted for a few moments about their upcoming trip and I smiled at the downright youthful way he talked about life now. I figure if I'm that happy when I retire I couldn't ask for much more in life.

Was anything really settled in the ongoing debate about my work vs settling down? Probably not, but at least we both understood the other's true wants and desires now. I realized he had noticeably avoided talk of Brandon. He had plans other than a blue-collar worker as my husband. *Family was never easy.*

I decided to call it a day a little early and go home to figure out dinner when a front desk customer service employee brought a dozen roses, yellow with flaming red tips displayed in a lovely cut glass vase. She placed them on my desk and wiggled her eyebrows. I couldn't keep a slight smile from forming and I knew I turned red. I opened the note. They were from Brandon and simply said "Hang in there KitKat. Devotedly yours." How sweet and thoughtful.

The phone rang and before I could say anything, Brandon quickly said, "I know you are emotionally spent, but I'm taking you out tonight to our favorite steak place to take your mind off everything and provide a reprieve. One pleasant evening of distraction." Brandon, my dear sweet Brandon. A girl couldn't do better than him. A heart of gold and so devoted.

Not like the new neighbor Mason, who I suspected had a string of gals in his life. Besides, I couldn't imagine him in a serious relationship. Okay, I was probably being unfair to compare them.

We agreed on the time he would pick me up for dinner and disconnected.

I snatched my purse with one hand and the vase with the other. I was done for the day and taking these roses home and show them off to Beverly and Delores.

Chapter Six

There was no sign of my neighbors, but my cousin Felicia was standing on my doorstep. She smiled and waved as I pulled up to the house. Although I love her, I suspected Brandon taking me out spurred her unexpected visit. *Okay, it may have been a few weeks since Brandon and I had spent much quality time together.* Still, it was just a little dinner out, a reprieve.

Felicia is the closest I ever came to having a sister. She is three years my junior, about five-foot-six, is a bit curvaceous and is one of those people who cheers up everyone she meets. Her style changes every few years, but she is the girly-girl with everything manicured, pedicured, painted, color coordinated, coifed, and hair-sprayed.

I was a wannabe next to her, lucky to paint my nails once a month, maybe. I enjoy simple elegance in clothes designs and jewelry. My first pearl necklace with matching earrings and bracelet I received upon high school graduation from dad are my favorite pieces.

We were sitting on my couch with plenty of time for a chat before Brandon was expected.

"Julie, I love you dear. You know that. But, I am telling you to get out more. You even have a guy to share moments with you." She paused and appeared to brace herself before continuing. "But, what do you do? You hide away and play your clarinet and go to work. If you love playing so much I don't know why you don't get on with the symphony. You know they would snatch you up after your temporary position with them." I was surprised. Felicia had never pushed me before, and this felt like she was trying to direct me.

"I don't want my clarinet to become my job. It would lose all its appeal then." I hugged her and she smelt of a light floral scent.

"I'm worried about you. Look honey, you need to go out tonight and enjoy yourself. You've had a rough week and you need to have some R&R. Just don't wear Brandon out, he is supposed to go on the last camping trip of the season with Loring this weekend so don't keep him up all night." Her smile was downright wicked.

"Felicia, that is none of your business, really." I think I blushed in every shade of red. Who knows, maybe tonight was just what I needed to distract my mind.

"What are you going to wear? Something to get the poor sap's heart racing?" Oh boy. She wanted to "help" me dress for dinner. I suspect this is one of her greatest pleasures in her life. She is always telling me I dress too conservatively. I like to call it classy, timeless and definitely not trendy.

"That's all well and good for work or business dinners, but not for a hot date. You have got to let your fun side out to play," Felicia often reprimanded. Consequently, she has been trying to spruce up my "party" clothes for the last few years. I contend she should work in the fashion industry rather than a coffee house barista, maybe then she would leave me alone.

I groaned. "Felicia, no. It's just dinner with Brandon. I wasn't planning on making an impact or getting his blood racing. I don't have it in me for wowing tonight."

She glared at me. "You, my dear cousin take Brandon for granted. Just because he's always there for dinner out doesn't mean he'll always be on call. Now get your butt up and let me dress you."

By the time she was done I was wearing a royal blue satin cowl neck top with a short black skirt and black strap heels. She had insisted on freshening my makeup (which I had not been wearing) and swooped my black hair up. I was always amazed at how effortlessly she could make me over. I looked into the mirror and barely recognized myself.

Brandon arrived shortly after Felicia told me to try and get some sleep before work, the naughty girl. Brandon, in navy Dockers, a cashmere pullover, and a splash of cologne let out an appreciative whistle and a huge grin spread on his face.

"You're stunning. I know you have to work tomorrow, I'll try to get you home before it gets too late." His voice held a promise of more, or maybe it was hope for more than just dinner. I wasn't sure how I felt about that prospect.

As I was settling into his respectable navy blue Toyota Corolla, I looked across the street to find Mason Sheridan leaving his home with a silky Sheltie prancing on a leash. He tipped an imaginary hat to me and directed his dog in the opposite direction. I was surprised to find that I was disappointed at his nonchalant reaction. After all, I was dressed to impress. Guess it didn't impress Bond Jr. with the models he no doubt had photographed.

Brandon took me to one of his favorite locally owned steak restaurants. We were greeted by the owners and seated. The subdued conversations and the soft lighting were welcoming. This was nice. I needed this.

We placed our orders. I selected the Chilean sea bass, which I love, and Brandon the prime rib along with the house wine.

"Julie, I may get a promotion at work. It isn't much, but I could be a shift manager. It would mean my working the midnight shift though." He expected me to comment, to give him permission I suppose.

"Brandon that's great. If that's what you want then that's great. I'm happy for you." I smiled. He worked at a local electronics plant since high school graduation. Nothing glamorous, but good pay and benefits.

"It may not be much, but I get a raise plus a shift differential.   I want to start putting some money away...for our future." His gaze was gentle and sincere. We had never talked about our "future" before.

"A promotion is fantastic. I hope to advance once I complete the training program. I won't always be the events and promotions director at the Resort." This wasn't going like I thought it would. What happened to my reprieve?

"Of course. Eventually, you'll move up and Chad won't always be there. I hope we can pay for the wedding and buy a house after we live at your townhome for a little and save up a good down payment. Of course, the sale of your townhome will help towards a larger home. We'll need enough room for children." He was holding my hand across the table.

Whoa, whoa, whoa! Hold on a flipping second. Was this his idea of a proposal, this oh so sensible discussion of our future? Had I heard him correctly? The room felt like it was closing in on me.

He expects me to settle down here when I've been working so hard to build my resume in resort management.   He knew my dreams, I'd talked to him many times about the places I wanted to travel and live. I think my mouth must have been hanging open because his brows scrunched together in question.

I closed my mouth and swallowed. "I suppose we'll rent out the house when I get resort jobs in foreign countries?" Let's just nip this in the bud right now. I felt my temper starting to rise. Perhaps before the murder I might have been patient, but now I wasn't ignoring the assumptions. I felt warm and looked around at the other diners, who seemed oblivious to our drama.

"Surely you've given up your childhood cruise ship fantasies. Life isn't The Love Boat. You've got a good job and we've been together long enough to know we're a good match." He took a deep breath. "I'm not saying this very well, I had hoped to be more romantic, more eloquent. I love you Julie and I think we're good for each other. Will you ma...."

"Stop Brandon." I threw a hand up like a crossing guard. I didn't care if people were looking now. "It isn't a matter of how eloquently you say it. My goals for my life aren't childhood fantasies." I realized the last few days had changed me. I was struggling to feel normal, myself again. This was too much. "My job is important to me and I'm working hard to realize my plans for my future. Apparently, that wasn't important as you planned the rest of my life without even asking me. You decided for me." I looked down at my lap and realized that Felicia must have known this would be more than just a dinner out and Brandon would propose tonight. That explained her dressing me up special.

"Julie, surely after the murder at work you understand managing a resort in a foreign country is a bigger job than you thought. You've got a good job and between us we can make a comfortable living and raise children here – not gallivanting around resort hopping." He clenched his jaw. We've known each other long enough for me to recognize he had it all mapped out in his mind and there was no changing it tonight.

The waitress brought our meals and we ate in silence. I couldn't tell you what it tasted it like. No dessert.

Brandon dropped me off at the curb a mere hour and a few minutes after picking me up and we didn't even say goodbye. *So much for my reprieve.* I stood at my door watching his car pull away, feeling empty. I blew out a shaky breath.

This looked bad for us. But, if I was honest with myself, I never saw myself married to Brandon. He had been in my life and part of the family for so long. We just were together. It had been comfortable, until now.

Perhaps I was guilty of not considering him in my future either. I had some thinking to do about where I saw him in my life. I owed Brandon that much.

"What're you doing home already and without taking your guy inside for a night cap?" *Great, just what I needed.* Bond Jr. was wheeling out a garbage can to the curb for pickup in the morning and had to rub it in. I didn't feel up to answering him.

He strolled over and stood three steps below me. His hair was disheveled from a soft breeze and several curly strands fell in his face. He reflexively ran his hand through his hair to restore order. Under the sparkling sky with a sickle moon winking, he was a walking dream. I swallowed. Moonlight was deceptive.

"Dinner didn't go so well. We.... He doesn't..." I stopped trying to talk as my throat began to close. I must be emotionally exhausted because I wasn't the crying type. I clenched my fists remembering how easily Brandon dismissed my dreams as silly fantasies. My eyes started to get moist. I leaned my back against my front door.

"He's clearly an idiot and doesn't have the slightest idea what he's doing. Am I close?" He had one foot resting on a step and his hands on his hips.

"You forgot how he trampled on my career and dreams or mapped out my future without asking me." I forced out while I could.

"Ahhh. He pulled the 'responsible male' act." He nodded. "Let me guess, he had the money all detailed out from the savings and house." He waved at my townhome that dad gave me.

"Yep." I squeaked.

"He plotted the course of your lives and the children you'd have." He studied me for several heartbeats, neither of us moving. "So how many children was he planning? Out of curiosity."

"A very practical three I believe were his thoughts." I sniffed. Brandon had mentioned that at some point in the evening. I think I cringed when he said it.

"He'll either realize he's about to lose something very dear to him with his controlling and planning and change his outlook to include your dreams, or he'll be stubborn and insist he's right. The question is what will you do?" The tears that had threatened were dry now.

"He's been in my life from junior high school since he's my cousin Loring's best friend and is pretty much a member of my family already. We started casually dating around a year ago, seemed natural. Now...it's complicated." The words just tumbled out. Perhaps it was because he was a stranger for the most part, but I was finding it easy to open up.

"Perhaps that's your problem. He's more like a brother, or cousin than he is a lover and partner." His words were kind and his voice like a caress. I looked at him a bit startled. He's more than a handsome face... and broad shoulders.

I nodded my head. "Maybe. You just may be correct in that... Mason."

He skipped up the few steps and kissed me lightly on the cheek, then whispered in my ear. "You look stunning by the way. He should've melted like butter at seeing you." My heart stopped for a few beats.

He turned and was jogging back to his house before I could say anything. That little inner voice said,

"Careful Julienne. That boy would never be happy with you." I scoffed, *where had that come from?* I had to figure out what to do about Brandon, not let a passing acquaintance with a neighbor distract me.

Chapter Seven

I was back in my office the next day, staring at the framed poster of Villa D'Este Lake Como in Italy surrounded by the Alps. I hoped to work there someday.

I had sulked the rest of the night, not able to settle on my clarinet or the latest historical novel. I ended up watching a travel show about Sri Lanka. I'd had a rough night after the argument with Brandon and the surprising chat with Bond Jr. My restlessness found its way into my sleep and dreams.

I struggled to get any energy together for work and only just made it on time.

Felicia called and got the brunt of my bad humor.

"You could've warned me, you know? I hold you partially responsible."

"What? The proposal turned into an argument. How is that even possible?" Bewilderment evident. "And don't blame me. How can two people get angry about taking it to the next logical level?" She huffed.

"Did you know he had planned out my life? That he thought my resort management plans were foolish fantasies?"

I got more irritated when she seemed more upset about Brandon's feelings than mine. After all, I'm the blood relative, thank you very much. No, I don't want to settle down and get on with making a family. *What is it with everybody lately?*

First, my dad expecting me to provide grand kids, then Brandon locking me into his life plan complete with three children.

"Felicia, I have to focus but we'll talk more later." I didn't want any more blasting my frustrations at her.

I barely got started on my unread emails when Chad walked in and slammed the newspaper down on my desk. The headline stared up at me, "Disgruntled Employee Suspected in Pastor's Slaying." I looked up at Chad confused.

"What disgruntled employee?"

"You. I suggest you read it now then tell me how I'm supposed to keep the reputation of the Colorado Springs Hotel and Resort from being ruined when you're implicated in the murder?" He spun around and stalked out of my office. *Oh crap.*

I read through the article in stunned silence. It fabricated a suspect, yours truly, along with evidence to implicate me. It relied heavily on my being the only person with the opportunity to stab Pastor Tom. I checked the byline only to find the article written by

Tiffany Davidson. I went to high school with a gal by that name. A sense of dread spread through me and settled in my gut. I thought of the reporter at the press conference who had seemed familiar and glared at me. Could the angry reporter and Tiffany, who I suspected from high school, be the same person? This was not going to turn out well.

The phone rang and I reluctantly answered it.

"Miss Julienne LaMere, I'm an attorney your father has retained to represent your interests. I think we need to talk since your name is in the paper now." His voice was mature, but I detected a New England twang that brought memories of the Kennedys to mind. *What great timing dad.* Mr. Chalmers advised me not to talk to any reporters or police again without his presence. *Like I would, I'm not gullible.* We scheduled to meet for lunch at the Resort's more casual restaurant.

I was very grateful that dad had jumped right on the lawyer. I'd forgotten all about it. The phone rang again. It was going to be one of those days.

"Two things princess. I see you're in the papers now and you turned down Brandon's proposal. I'll be in town tomorrow, I couldn't get a flight out today." Dad.

"No, don't!" I felt like a teenager again. "I still have to go to work. You'll probably talk to me more on the phone than if you came here." It may seem that any good loving daughter would be happy for a visit, but this was a strategic maneuver to ensure my life complied with his game plan. After the close call with

Brandon planning my future, I didn't want to go there with Dad. Not now. Not with everything else going on, I could only juggle so much.

"Princess, I'm not going to be sitting by while you need family around you. I'll stay with Regina and Lars so you don't have to put me up." It was a nice thought but this was about more than a family huddle.

"Dad, I'm not going to change my mind about Brandon even if you come out. Brandon and I have very different things we want out of life. Besides, he doesn't make near the money you expect me to marry." I was hoping we could have the argument now and he would cancel his travel plans.

"Brandon is already practically family, I know he will take good care of you..."

"He won't make me happy. I'm not going to marry a man just to please everybody else." I held my breath for his response.

"That'll change, you don't know what you want. Look at your clinging to that ridiculous job after your name is connected to a murder. You should've quit that job months ago. Just marry Brandon. Real life isn't love-at-first-sight, heart-racing romance. Now I'll take care of everything..." He wasn't listening, again. Did I need to be more forceful? Adamant?

"Dad, I'm asking you not to fly out. I love you. You did everything when Mom died, but if you insist on coming out here with the sole purpose to orchestrate my life, I'll take a vacation and not be here." I was afraid to stop or he would take over the conversation again.

"I don't know how much clearer I can be. You need to deal with your own life. You put your life on hold while you raised me and now you need to live your life some." I took a breath and he didn't jump in.

"The lawyer called me, I'm meeting with him in a few hours. If things look serious, I'll call you and we'll discuss a visit. But I mean it, dad. No more playing chess with my life, planning the next five moves."

Silence. I had my fingers crossed. Finally, my father took a deep breath and spoke. "Well if that's how you feel, I guess I don't have a choice." This was the first time I had really put my foot down and got him to listen. But, I didn't like it. I knew he'd think I didn't need him or something like that. We hung up soon after that.

I needed a stiff drink, but I wasn't likely to get anything till after work. I squared my shoulders and started for Chad's office, I might as well use my forceful momentum while I had it, I had no idea when it would evaporate.

I knocked on Chad's office door and waited to hear the distinct "Enter."

He motioned for me to sit down but I couldn't. My instincts told me that things were going from bad to worse and I was caught in the rush, no longer able to control the direction.

"I understand how all this may look, but I didn't kill Pastor Drake, I haven't been arrested and ..." His phone rang and he gave me the raised index finger to wait.

"What do you mean....Where? Look, pranks are not..." His face drained of color and he swallowed. He slowly hung up but picked the receiver back up. "Ron, I just had a caller say there was a bomb in the hotel to avenge Pastor Drake's murder." He looked directly at me with a glint of anger.

He slammed the phone into the cradle then stood up and moved into the hallway.

"Should we pull the fire alarm, that'll get everybody outside the fastest?" I suggested.

"You're to go home, take the rest of the day off. I'll call you tonight." He pulled the alarm and took off at a run. Well, at least I still had a job, *I think*. If the hotel was still standing.

I grabbed my purse and the newspaper then locked up my office. This hadn't been my week. I walked home past a fire engine screaming toward the hotel feeling trampled and a failure. I called Mr. Chalmers and arranged to meet at my house instead of at the hotel restaurant.

Once home, I made myself a grilled cheese with Swiss and pumpernickel and a side of cole slaw I had in the fridge from the deli while I watched the news coverage. Just one news station was covering the situation. I was on auto pilot. I was upset that I wasn't there doing my job and assisting Chad, but I was somewhat glad to not be splashed on TV right now. I had enough attention with the newspaper article.

The bomb squad had gone through the hotel building and nothing was found. The police stated they would investigate the false call that alerted resort management of the bomb. Then the reporter talked to guests, who were mixed in their responses between inconvenienced and hostile over the situation.

Mr. Chalmers "Esquire" arrived precisely on time and asked questions. I answered and he took notes. He was in his fifties, gray at the temples, average looking but dripping with money. His shirt was monogrammed, diamond cuff links and tie pin, Rolex watch. I hope he was worth whatever dad was paying him.

"I'm afraid I might lose my job over this murder when I did nothing wrong, as it is I was sent home when the bomb threat was phoned in rather than help."

"I think a phone call to the resort General Manager will take care of that." He patted my hand like my dad might have. "You must do an excellent job and not give them any excuse for dismissal, if they do – they'll be sorry." He smiled a tight half smile meant to reassure me but it failed.

After Mr. Chalmers left I turned my phone back on. I sent a group text message to Felicia, Aunt Regina, Uncle Lars, my best friend Porsche (I needed to update her on Brandon), and even a few neighbors to let them all know I was okay and the bomb threat was a false alarm according to the news.

The phone rang as I was skimming the newspaper article once again by Tiffany Davidson that declared I was the most likely suspect. The voice on the phone was blaring and I held it away.

"You haven't called me, you haven't told me what happened with that pompous Pastor Drake and now there was a bomb threat. You've been holding out on me and I'm going to require a lot of kissing up to get over it, honey."

That's my best friend Porsche. We've been friends since junior year of high school when she was the new girl just moved here from New York and nobody liked her outspoken ways. We bonded over cafeteria food, varsity volleyball, and study hall. We stayed close throughout her going off to college for her degree in history. She's an Associate Professor at Colorado College, the prestigious liberal arts college in town.

"I've been trying to work through all this in my head, I meant to tell you everything. I've got huge news about Brandon too..."

"Hold on, this is not something to dump on me over the phone with a murder and relationship news. I can pick up Chinese on the way over and we can get some serious girl time in."

"I'll make up your favorite chocolate mousse with the touch of chili powder real quick for us too. I am so glad you called." And I was. I could tell Porsche everything and she would say what she thought and have me laughing in no time. I really wanted to know if she knew anything about Pastor Tom from her students too.

It's just a teensy weensy bit of research as a self-preservation tactic. I might even do some internet background on Pastor Tom. I needed to feel a bit more in control of the situation rather than tossed on the waves, and knowledge was power. Or something like that.

Chapter Eight

We didn't need a formal neighborhood watch, we had our unique version. My neighbors had eagle eyes. I walked to the mailboxes by the clubhouse and admired the colorful shrubbery clothed in fall glory that sprinkled the park-like landscaping. Two large oaks that sporadically floated leaves in a graceful offering shaded the centrally located mailboxes. Beverly and Nathan a retired white-haired Doctor who keeps an eye on the neighborhood joined me in seconds.

"Tell us all about it." Nathan eyed me, checking to see if I was in one piece probably.

"Not much to tell, newspaper says I'm most likely Drake's killer, a bomb threat was phoned into the hotel, bomb squad was called and I was sent home. I'm hoping I still have a job, and a career, let alone not jailed for murder when this is all over. What've you guys heard?"

"Only what has been on the news and what you've told me." Beverly offered.

"I don't like it. This whole affair's peculiar. Pastor Drake had so many people lined up to punch him in the face you could sell tickets, but you're the one on the hot seat. Did you know him at all?" Nathan ran a hand over his neatly trimmed white beard and mustache. He was a retired surgeon and former M.A.S.H. doctor from Vietnam who kept active.

"Nope. I knew of him, like most people around here, but I'd never met the guy before. What about you? It sounds like you knew him?" I crossed my fingers and toes hoping I would hear something to assure me I wasn't the only suspect.

"I know a few doctors who knew him. From all accounts, he was a piece of work. Rumors say he was into some kinky sex. Plus, I heard his business partner was getting a lawyer 'cause he was taking over the radio program and shutting him out. Like I said, peculiar." He had a scowl on his mouth and fire in his elderly eyes.

I shivered, not from the temperate air that held a whisper of chill, but the topic we discussed. It was surreal amid the gentle beauty surrounding us.

"He's got a radio show, too? What wasn't the guy involved in?   Got that huge church and wrote that book, he's on that cable news show all the time spouting his mouth off. Radio too, well, well." Beverly was shaking her head.

I had to agree with her. He was the hot religious figure of the moment and had run with it and some might say milked it. His church had something like ten thousand or more members and his last book, *In Your Face Gospel*, generated a lot of attention...and controversy.

"What do you mean people would line up to punch him?" I wasn't letting that juicy bit go without discussion.

"Just that he made a few enemies...and I think he was a swinger." Nathan stared down at his worn loafers and a little pink blossomed on his ears.

"Swinger, as in wife swapping, hanging-from-the chandeliers swinger? How do you know that?" My voice was low but I couldn't help but sound skeptical. I found it difficult to fathom in this conservative bastion. I suppose there's a danger of the wild side busting loose when a person is too repressed. Not that I would know anything about that.

"Well, like I said, I know some docs that know him. One of them was invited by Pastor Drake to join several couples one evening. He made a point of saying the parties were a monthly thing and lasted all night if he and his wife were open to new experiences." His ears were turning bright red and his eyes were locked on the ground.

"He said he wanted to get to know my friend's wife better. My friend was positive that good ole Pastor Drake had a monthly wife swap going."

"How could something like that not have gotten out?" Beverly protested and I nodded. *Yeah, how?*

"Because these were all influential people involved, none of them wanted that sort of scandal getting out. People keep that stuff quiet no matter who's involved."

"Anything else? Because I need to give something to the police and get them off my back."

"Nothing solid, just gossip. Let's just say I wouldn't be surprised at any kinky thing that may come out about the dearly departed Padre. But no, I have no more particulars." He shrugged his shoulders.

I walked back to my house. I could see a cute Sheltie looking out with his ears perked up at Mason's front picture window, signs of a dog waiting for his person to come home. Roulette I surmised. I guess Bond Jr. wasn't so bad if he had earned the devotion of a dog, right? You never hear of playboys fussing over their beloved pet.

I had just enough time to whip up the mousse and get a little internet research on Pastor Tom before Porsche was due with our dinner.

Chapter Nine

Within only fifteen minutes I had printed out several pages of information on Pastor Tom. I decided to break out a bottle of Chardonnay that should go well with what I knew would be the Chinese menu items Porsche would bring. I added the Pinot Noir from the wine rack for the beef dishes. That should cover the bases.

I got dishes and utensils ready when I noticed Porsche outside laughing. A quick glance out my floor to ceiling windows told me she had discovered Mason. *This ought to be interesting.* I slipped out to join them and play hostess.

Porsche reached out as she laughed and grazed her hand along his arm. Mason spotted me and smiled.

"Howdy neighbor."

I performed the standard introductions next to her car. "Mason, this is Porsche my best friend since high school. Porsche, my new neighbor Mason Sheridan."

"Mason Sheridan... your name sounds familiar. What do you do?" Porsche was deciding whether he was worth her time. She was tall, poised, and pretty in that sophisticated way. And blonde, did I mention she was blonde? The combination ensured she had plenty of dates. But, she was like a cat that played with a toy until the novelty wore off and she moved on to the next one. One of these days she would surely find a guy who was a keeper, but not so far. She still had her hand on his arm, like old friends.

"Photographer mostly." He flashed a dazzling smile, bright and full of mischief. "Come out and play," it said and his eyes promised he would make it worth her while. *Oh yeah, I wouldn't have to worry about Mason giving me a second look anymore.*

"I think I know your work." She purred. I grabbed the bags of Chinese food and was about to go wait in the house for these two to finish when she surprised me. "Isn't your father General Sheridan, commander of the Air Force Space Command?" I stopped dead in my tracks. My eyebrows had to be half way up my forehead. *Well, that was something.* Didn't most General's sons follow in dad's footsteps?

"Yeah, he's my Dad. But I'll warn you, he may not claim me." He winked and the smile quirked up one side. He was working it. Porsche let her eyes scan his button down shirt, designer jeans, and down to his shoes.

I left them and took the food inside. I was unloading and getting serving spoons for everything when she finally joined me. No doubt she'd gotten his phone number and they would go out on at least one date, maybe more. I'd hear all about it, probably more than I wanted to know about my neighbor.

Before I could even hand her a plate she surprised me.

"Did I make you mad without knowing it? 'Cause you didn't call me about Pastor Drake, then I find a cross between Hugh Jackman and Aidan Turner moved in next door and you definitely didn't share that with me either."

I rolled my eyes in answer.

"Unleeeeess you like tall, dark, and steamy next door for yourself?" Her eyebrows were raised in question.

"Don't be ridiculous, he's not my type."

"Are you breathing? How can he *not* be every woman's secret fantasy?" She let out a protracted sigh with a slight moan at the end. Dear Porsche hadn't changed since high school when she read every romance novel with the bad boy leading man.

We sat on my overstuffed navy blue sofa and ate with smooth jazz playing in the background. Between bites of sesame chicken, Kung Pao beef, and Mongolian barbeque with sides of egg rolls and chow mien I told her everything from the last few days.

"Pastor Drake assaulted you and then had the gall to say he would get you fired? He's lucky you just kneed him. But, he got his comeuppance in the end." She took a delicate swallow of her wine. "Plus you're a suspect and the newspaper thinks you're the killer."

"That sums it up.   Can you imagine *me* killing anybody? Even that toad. It's just a freakish nightmare." I let that sit for a few seconds in silence.   "Hey, speaking of that article, it's written by Tiffany Davidson. Didn't we go to high school with a girl by that name?" Porsche had more friends than I did by senior year because she was in so many activities.

Her brows scrunched up, then her eyes grew big. "Oh.   Oh, no. Tiffany was the girl that Jessie Framns stood up to take you to the Sophomore homecoming dance. She hated you for that...really hated you. If it's the same gal, she's probably targeting you just for payback."

"I didn't know Jessie was dating anybody. I can see how she would be mad, but he stood me up the next dance. Shouldn't she be ticked at him, not me?" It was hard to believe that could possibly be the reason for condemning me as a killer in print. I removed my shoes and curled my legs next to me on the couch.

"What're you going to do? The lawyer is reassuring, but it doesn't get the real killer behind bars. This doesn't look good for you." She stabbed a forkful of Mongolian beef.

"Since you brought it up, I thought I'd do some initial research on good old Pastor Tom." I grabbed the printouts from the side table and began summarizing what I had found.

"He started out with a small church meeting in his home and grew it from there until the number of members supported buying a building. His following kept getting bigger until they built that large church they're in now. His radio ministry was looking at expanded syndication and rumor was the partner he started the radio program with wasn't included in the new deal. Nathan, my neighbor in number sixteen, mentioned the partner got a lawyer and I found a short article mentioning that. That's at least one other person with a motive. I plan on checking the attendees to the networking event and see if the partner was there."

"Interesting start, anything else?"

"I was kind of hoping you could ask other teachers and maybe some students if they know any reason somebody would kill him. His church has a big college outreach group and I thought you may have some in your classes." I held my breath.

"I can quietly ask my teaching assistant and a few students who are pretty open to me and see what they have to say. What're you looking for?" She took another mouthful. She was blessed with a metabolism that matched her appetite, unlike my yo-yo weight battle.

"I overheard somebody at work say he was into younger...young women and then Nathan said he knows a doctor who was invited by Pastor Tom to join a monthly swinger's party. I'd like to know if either can be verified in some way." I sat my plate on the side table. My appetite was suffering.

"No kidding? The right reverend was leading a double life filled with swinger's parties and younger gals. In that case, I'll connect with the counselors and ask some of the professors too. If the rumors are true, there are plenty of people who probably wanted to pay him back."

I was betting the poor wife was the first on that list.

"Plus, I need to find out how to get to the reception after the funeral." I held up the newspaper. "It's supposed to be tomorrow night by invitation only. I want to be a fly on the wall and hear what's said about the man."

"I don't know about that, but I know a caterer in town. I can ask if it is being catered and who has the job. You might work just the one job if they need the help." A catered funeral reception?

"I hadn't thought of that. I imagine they expect a big crowd with his national status and need the extra help. How soon can you find out?" I jumped on the idea since I hadn't come up with any other ideas how to crash the reception without risking ending up a news item.

"I can call and leave a message tonight and hopefully get back to you in the morning with an answer. Let me guess, you're going to dig some other suspects up to throw at the police?"

I nodded.

She set her empty dish down and held her wine glass with both hands. She got her no-nonsense face on. "Now, what about Brandon?" I was hoping she'd forgotten about that.

"He proposed and I said no. It was horrible." I held my hand up to stop her as she started to speak. "He had my life all mapped out and it didn't include travel or working anywhere else." I swallowed and continued in a near whisper. "He expected me to jump on the family-go-round highway and...change for him. You know how I feel about that." I was staring at the couch fabric.

She hugged me close for a minute then asked, "Do you love him, hun?"

I rubbed my eyes. "I love him, but the last several months it's been more like he's part of the family and not...a lover or partner." She didn't need to know those were Mason's words. But it was true, the more I thought about it the more I could see it now. I needed to tell Brandon how I felt.

"Oh, so you guys haven't been getting much sack time together and growing apart." Leave it to Porsche to put it in such harsh terms. Oh geez, I hope that wasn't how Mason translated it in his mind. But then again, why would I care what he thought?

"Umm, well..." How do you say the magic was gone without sounding like you still believed in the tooth fairy?

"There's no use fighting for something if it's dead. If there were some embers or spark I would encourage you to work on him and see if he can be won over to some sensitivity. It doesn't sound like you have any spark left for him." That summarized the situation neatly. Porsche's eyes got serious.

"Oh honey, I didn't know you were on the market when I agreed to a date with tall, dark, and yummy across the way. I can totally back off if you want a little rebound fling. Probably just what you need, somebody to get your fires stoked." She licked her lips and her eyebrows danced a jig.

"No, not necessary." I countered. She gave me the don't-bull-shit-me look. "Really. I don't want a playboy. He's out of my league, I'm not into players. You're free to play." I wiggled my fingers in a scurry along motion.

"Brandon was reliable and safe." She snapped her fingers. "But, you so need to have a steamy fling to shake your world up a bit."

I'm not a Bond girl. I repeated, even if only to myself. I'm not going there. Seriously. Not. Going. There.

Chapter Ten

Even with the crisper air tinged with the enticing smell of a fireplace, I was nervous when I walked to work the next morning. Chad never called as he said he would, thus I was unsure what to expect. I was early again in hopes of avoiding too many eyes if I was called into Chad's office over the swirling scandal I found myself in the middle of... or the worst scenario of losing my job.

I reached my office to find the door slightly open. I was positive I had closed up and locked it yesterday when I vacated from the bomb threat. Chad or facility maintenance must have needed to enter as part of the sweep for explosives. I looked around and nothing seemed missing or disturbed. Ever since...you know, everything has felt off. My office was less a happy part of my future but a constant reminder of the ugly side of life.

Enough of that. Today I was going to get a jump on some of the resort and golf member appreciation events to bolster our flagging reputation. I had some ideas already formulating and I wanted to have plans to present to Chad.

But I didn't have the chance. Chad appeared at my door and waved me into his office without a word. *Uh oh.*

I sat and attempted to breathe calmly, but I couldn't stop my hands from fidgeting. He closed the door. *Breathe Julie, breathe.*

"After I dealt with the bomb squad and answered all of the police questions, I had a chat with a Mr. Chalmers. I was surprised to find out you got a lawyer." His voice had progressively gotten louder and he had balled his hands into fists. I had forgotten Mr. Chalmers had said he would call Chad.

"Actually, my father got the lawyer after that newspaper article." I hated how that made me sound like a daddy's girl.

He took several deep breaths with his eyes closed. I could imagine him counting to ten.

"Look, I wasn't going to fire you. But, this whole situation better get cleared up fast or it'll be out of my hands." He pinched the bridge of his nose. "That article sparked a flurry of complaints from members. Even if they don't go to Pastor Drake's church, they want your head."

I felt the blood drain from my face and my chest tighten making it hard to breathe. I could practically hear my career swirling around, about to be flushed down the toilet. That was aside from whether I was arrested.

"I'm telling you, the way they talk about him is like he's some sort of martyr and you are the devil who slew him. Members... want you fired."

The members I had been developing and growing. The Colorado Springs Hotel and Resort is unusual in that we developed a membership along the lines of a country club to sustain us through the winter months when skiing took tourists to the mountains and golfers were not as plentiful. Membership wasn't cheap, but it was prestigious. My primary job was to foster, nurture, promote, and grow that membership as well as learn the marketing and management aspects of the business. I felt like the people I had been "nurturing" just betrayed me.

"Chad, I'll work hard. But I didn't do anything. I just met the man, I had no reason to impale him." Even to my ears, it sounded like I was begging. *Yeah, okay. I was begging.* I had fought my dad for this job, I had broken up with Brandon because this job was a step toward working resorts around the world. Now it was in jeopardy. You would beg too, I know you would.

"I'll do everything I can to help the police find who did this. That's all I can promise. I'll help resolve this." At least my voice was stronger this time.

"Don't do anything stupid Julienne. I don't need your father suing me because you do find the killer and got yourself hurt." I considered asking what I wanted for a half second and then just blurted it out.

"I was wondering if there's a way I can get into the Drake reception this evening? If it's catered or bartenders rented I'll work it." I held my breath after the words slipped out. He could forbid me to get involved.

"I don't think you should really get involved any further, it could backfire. But, I'll make a few phone calls. I'll disavow any knowledge of you if it goes sideways?" He licked his lips and swallowed. I think he was scared. "You'd better put your hair up and wear glasses. Try to look drab and forgettable. I don't need members calling because somebody recognizes you."

I looked at my office with different eyes. I didn't want to lose what I had worked and fought for. I knew I was lucky to get this on-the-job training. Everywhere I went in the resort I had a fuller appreciation of how fortunate I was and resolved to do whatever I could to keep my job and clear my name.

Mid morning I finally got an answer about Pastor Tom's funeral reception when Porsche phoned.

"Hey girlfriend, thanks for last night. I needed that."

"I'm a necessary part of your life, too long without exposure is bad for your emotional health. Didn't you know that?" I chuckled.

"That works both ways my friend." We both worked hard, but she tended towards work-a-holic.

"Can't talk long dear, but I have some news that couldn't wait." Porsche informed me who was handling the catering and had the name and number of the manager for me to contact.

"Great, I'll call immediately and see if they still need help. You rock."

"Oh, I'm not finished. I spoke to a few professors who said, without any student names, that the rumors of Pastor Tom's questionable attention to teens in his church were prevalent and they personally suspected they were true. A counselor hinted it was true in at least one case, but couldn't really share anything told in confidence." Her voice was triumphant.

"I can't help feel sorry for these girls. Thanks for all the information, that was fast."

"I have a class to teach, gotta run. I'll let you know if I find out anything more." With that she hung up.

I called the caterer immediately and was told they could use the extra help if I didn't mind walking with a tray of food. How swanky could it be? Since it was short notice, they faxed me some paperwork to fill out and said a uniform would be waiting at their office when I came to join the crew at four thirty to be driven out there. It was a whirlwind, but I was going undercover at the funeral reception. Still wasn't sure it was a good idea, but I had to do something to clear my name I couldn't sit on the side lines any longer.

I ran out on my lunch and bought some cheap glasses from a costume shop downtown. The selection was limited so I settled for the horn-rimmed glasses that were common in the fifties. Surely nobody would recognize me in those if I pulled my hair back.

I was anxious the rest of the afternoon and clocked out in time to walk home and put my hair up. I would put the glasses on at the last minute. With sensible shoes on, my hair in a French bun, and a quickly made peanut butter and jam sandwich to go I drove off, passing Mason walking his dog. I waved and smiled as a good neighbor does and then put him out of my head.

I had to focus. Thoughts of Mason with his dark chocolate wavy hair tumbling to his shoulders and cleft chin with Porsche were only making my head hurt. *What did I care anyway, he wasn't my type.* He was a playboy and wasn't likely to change.

I turned my thoughts to the reception. My internet research had provided me with photos of his church staff and wife plus their three children. I felt like I could at least understand who most of the main players would be. I had a small pocket notebook to take notes before forgetting any unfamiliar names.

I drove on autopilot with thoughts whizzing through my head. This was the most impulsive act I had ever done. Plus, I had never waitressed, unlike all my friends in high school over summer break. I was too busy at Band Camp and Youth Symphony Music Camp playing the clarinet.

Once I arrived at the caterers it was frenzied activity. I got my uniform and it was loose and a tad long in the skirt so that helped the dumpy look and the glasses topped it off. I was rather proud of my disguise. I slipped the notebook in the skirt pocket.

The staff piled into a van with a few cars loaded up as well and headed to an upscale part of town with newer pricey homes. We pulled into the drive of a two story with a basement on a huge lot and pulled around to the back. For the next hour, I helped setup in the kitchen and make platters to be circulated.

Apparently, Pastor Tom made some good money because the kitchen had two refrigerators, two ovens, and two dishwashers plus a professional grade 5-burner stove top.

It seemed no time at all before Sarah – Pastor's widow and the children arrived with several other adults that I guessed were relatives. Sarah looked pale and her eyes were red and swollen, but she critically surveyed the preparations and made some changes here and there. She looked right at me without pausing. I breathed a sigh of relief that she didn't suspect I was the alleged killer from the newspaper. Fortunately, the article hadn't had any photos. If I ever doubted wait staff were invisible at such events it was confirmed now, or my disguise was better than I expected.

Once I left the kitchen, and got my first view of the living room I nearly let out a whistle. Cathedral ceilings and stone tile floors with cavernous space. The living room was at least two thousand square feet. I would be exhausted tonight after just a few circuits. The furniture was Chippendale replicas in shades of dusty rose to Merlot. The artwork was actual oil paintings with gold gilt frames, all of Biblical themes. Restrained excess was the decorating style, as if this family wanted badly to impress but didn't want to shriek "fleecing the flock."

Crowds of people were filing into the house and I was making slow progress in my rounds with trays of food. The noise levels remained subdued to a hum, so I was able to catch snippets of conversations as I passed.

The press of bodies was like swimming upstream in every direction and the mix of clashing and competing perfumes was oppressive. Several children were darting through the crowd chasing each other, making my job precarious. The sluggish progress across the room was ideal for me to catch conversations without appearing to be listening in, and to pop a bite from my tray here and there.

I was on the edges surveying the masses when I saw the widow Sarah duck into a side room with a man and shut the door. *Interesting.*

It was a challenge to pick my way around people with my tray held up. My arms were already aching. If I made it through the night without dropping a few trays on any heads or toes it would be a miracle. I reached the door the good widow had entered to find it ajar. Nobody seemed aware of my existence, so I stood with my ear close to the opening and tried to appear as though I was arranging the food on the tray.

I could see a sliver of the room, Sarah seemed to be pacing, then it stopped. I caught only faint voices. I took a deep breath and sauntered into the room as if this were part of my route.

Sarah was in a man's arms. I suddenly recognized him as the man who helped her through her initial shock at the luncheon. I would have dismissed it as consoling the grief-stricken except for the smeared lipstick and bright eyes of the widow. I didn't recognize the man from the church website or other research around Pastor Tom's life. *Very curious.*

"Pardon me, hors d'oeuvres?"

"This is an off limits room, please leave and shut the door." Sarah fired off as she turned her back toward me. I tried to commit the man's face to memory then shrugged in apology and left, closing the door. *The evening was starting out well.* Even with the intimate scene, it didn't seem passionate when I walked in. They weren't kissing, no roving hands, or looking into each other's eyes, just holding each other. Still, there very well could be a motive for murder there.

I surveyed the scene for my next target. I would barely have enough on my tray for a short circuit before needing to restock.

I recognized the Youth Minister from the church's website and locked on him. Robert Crandel had been hired for the position two years ago so I was taking a chance that a relative newcomer would know much dirt dump. He was talking to a group.

"...detective says he can't discuss an ongoing investigation. We called the DA, even the Mayor and nobody can get him to say what progress they've made." Crandel finished.

"It's hard to believe some low wage employee would've killed him. Seems he'd been making enough people mad who knew him for an outsider to snap." This comment was from a prim and proper sweater-set blond woman. *Was she talking about me?*

"Don't look at me. Tom and I got along fine, no complaints here." Crandel's monotone held no conviction.

"Just drama from a few teen girls who thought they were Tom's special project to find out they're the latest in a long line of projects. I don't mind saying I wondered about his attention to the girls, they weren't Eliza Doolittle for Pete's sake." A man holding a squirming toddler volunteered.

"I was always grateful my daughter was away at college. They can be so impressionable at that age, easily developing a crush on a godly man of influence. I'm sure that's all there was to it. That Cindy, Cathy, or whatever her name was that killed herself can't be blamed on Tom. Bob, I know you look after our youth like they're your own." The man with the perfectly swept back hair looked hard at Crandel.

"I'd do what needed to be done to protect our children." Crandel's eyes developed a stern appearance.

But, would he murder to stop Pastor Tom from taking advantage of an impressionable girl. What was the story behind this poor forgettable girl Cindy, or Cathy?

I had to move on since the man with toddler noticed me loitering. I tried to navigate to the David Babcock, Tom's business partner, who seemed to be holding court rather than mourning.

"I'm just sick over the loss of a faithful warrior. Tom's murder just proves the forces of darkness fighting to silence the good news. You're taking up the banner and continuing to fight for the kingdom aren't you?" spoke a lady wearing another sweater-set and color-coordinated shoes, necklace, and earrings. Her expertly styled hair was clearly professionally colored.

"I've placed a phone call to see about salvaging the show for the sake of the ministry and the listeners. I'd be a logical choice but I can't speak for board of directors and new syndication partner, naturally. I'll provide my aid to keep the radio ministry going even if we don't get the expanded syndication." Babcock was smooth. He didn't give any hint of what my research online had revealed. Could he have killed to keep his radio celebrity that Pastor Tom was jeopardizing?

From my research I found good old Tom knew nothing about radio and ratings, but David Babcock started him out, taught him how to build an audience, how to put on a show with drama, not just a Bible lecture. The general consensus was that Pastor Tom would never have become a sensation if it weren't for Babcock mentoring him and building the radio empire. But the new expanded syndication contract negotiations were rumored to have cut Babcock out. I suspected that was motive enough. With Tom out of the way, David Babcock could step right in as the new face of the program and be a hero saving the radio ministry.

My tray was empty and I started the trek back to the kitchen to fill up with more food. I looked towards the kitchen door and nearly dropped my tray. Tiffany Davidson, the reporter who glared at me during the press conference at the Resort, and who had painted me in the papers as the likely killer was scrutinizing the crowd. I remembered her from high school now.

Memories flooded back. She was in marching band with me, and I seem to remember her angling to date Brandon after the Jessie Framn's fiasco. Back then, Brandon was at my Uncle Lars and Aunt Regina's place with my cousin Loring regularly. He seemed happy to take me to dances occasionally so he could tag along with Loring.

She was pretty in a no-frills sense but had developed more confidence than her high school self who always sought validation from boys. Or she was just incredibly competitive with other girls. I do remember her being serious in several sports.

Whether Tiffany still held a grudge or not, she did hold a camera and was raising it to take some pictures.

I veered to the left to swing around and get to the kitchen in a wide arc ending behind her.

I wanted to stay in the kitchen as long as possible. I'm a die-hard chicken and I was avoiding Tiffany and her camera. I loaded my tray, asked the supervisor some questions, got a drink of water. I eventually had to just get it over with. I lifted my full tray loaded with bar-b-que cocktail hot dogs and found Tiffany had moved. I scanned the crowd so I could keep out of a photo if possible.

This time I decided on a group of people that I didn't recognize from any of my research and wondered if they might have different information. I was surrounded by expressions of sympathy for the widow and children.

"So much sorrow. First Sarah...well, I hear she was inconsolable and about to leave Tom, then that poor Cynthia went running back to her folks in Seattle and killed herself. How her folks must have wept. Now Pastor Tom has been taken from his work too young. The world is too full of misery." I looked at the speaker to find a grandmother type with sincerity and sorrow in her eyes speaking to what seemed to be her husband and daughter.

"People doing things they ought not to be doing only brings sorrow. We haven't learned a thing over the centuries." Her husband stated simply.

I scanned the crowd again and spotted Tiffany and her camera ready to take a picture. I spun and disappeared into the crowd. I continued to elude the camera for a couple more hours and several trays of food. My feet were hurting and swollen by the time the crowds left and everything was cleaned and packed up. In the van, I just listened to the tales from the other servers about the gossip surrounding Pastor Tom. Not a hint anywhere of a swingers group, but plenty of tales along the same lines as what I had already gathered.

I hadn't had a chance to write anything in my little notebook and now it would look too obvious in front of the others.

I soaked my feet in Epsom salts the instant I was home. Before I collapsed into bed, I texted Porsche to ask her if she could find anything about a Cynthia from Seattle from students. Just maybe a student who attended Drake's church would have known her. When Porsche didn't text me back I had to force myself not to think about her on a date with Mason and focus on what I had gathered so far on the murder. I fell into a sound sleep quickly.

Chapter Eleven

I was on the job and had gone through my files, positive I had printed out the attendees for the fatal networking event. But, I couldn't find it in any folder. I remembered my office door had been unlocked yesterday and wondered if anybody could have removed the list. I suppose Chad could have gotten it for the police. I didn't want to sound paranoid, so I kept repeating to myself there was a simple explanation.

I then turned to my email to find the file sent by the event organizer with the luncheon attendance list. After a few minutes, I was able to locate the email and printed off another copy.

I had listed the suspects thus far in my little notebook. Widow Sarah, the business partner David Babcock, the youth director Robert Crandel, Seattle Cynthia's family seemed an outside shot, and perhaps a jilted lover in the swinger's group - either a woman or a man jealous or jilted by Tom. There was no guarantee that I was even remotely close, but this would at least give the police more than just me.

But, they needed not only motive but the opportunity too. The person responsible had to be at the Convention Center. I started comparing my suspects to the list. I remembered Robert Crandel was there, but it seemed Sarah and the business partner also attended. Well, the more suspects the better at this point.

Of course, I didn't know yet who were regulars in the swingers group...if there was a swingers group. I still wasn't completely convinced about that. It seemed so outlandish for our town. But, if Pastor Tom had been in a swinger's group, wouldn't that suggest his wife was too? Could that mystery man holding the widow at the reception be involved in any such group and that's how they were close? I added *mystery man* to my list of suspects.

I stopped in my tracks, what about the church secretary? I remember an old comedy sketch about how the church lady knew everything in the church. I smiled. Bet Pastor Tom's secretary was the keeper of a few secrets. I could find out a lot from her...if she would talk to me, at least about the time Sarah spent at her folks and if there were marital problems as the one grandmotherly guest had hinted. Maybe even elaborate on Seattle Cynthia.

I turned to my computer and went to the church website. No bio of the secretary like they had posted for the assistant pastor, youth director, and others.

Hmmm. I wasn't sure how to proceed from here. But whatever I did, it needed to appear innocent.

If Nathan knew about the swinger connection, I wondered if some of the Resort Shadows community had contacts with the church? It looked like I would be walking home for lunch to chat with my conspiring neighbors.

While I was at the search engine, my fingers typed in the name Mason Sheridan. I want the record to reflect that my fingers acted on their own volition, I had no conscious part in it. I found he was a good photographer. The landscapes were beautiful and I think I recognized some of them from calendars.

There were a few references to him in celebrity news as being linked with an actress or model, but they were small notices and never twice with the same person. That either meant he didn't date them for long, he dated other players, or just maybe they weren't the romantic dates the press made them out to be. *Ha. Yeah, right. Who am I kidding?* All those gossipy news items were more than a year old too, nothing recent.

There was one notice about his playing in a high stakes poker game and the money he walked away with took my breath away. The photo of him at the poker table was a cool, shrewd, and confident man, not the charming neighbor I had met. It was that small poker notice that mentioned he was prior Marine Special Forces and attributed his nerves of steel at the table to his training. Marine Special Forces didn't compute with Bond Jr. and his full curly locks...although he has an aura that you don't want to cross him. The more I learned, the more he was a murky enigma.

I already did some advance preparation for the Thanksgiving Feast we were offering members in a month. I had flyers to design, get approved by Chad, and mail out. I wanted to include in the mailing any special the Resort restaurants and shops might be planning for that time frame as well, so I sent out an email to the retail network.

I called Porsche in between work tasks.

She answered with a brusque "Hello, Porsche." *Late night last night?*

"Hope I'm not calling at a bad time. Just wanted to check in with you." I held my breath.

She exhaled a deep sigh, "No, it's fine. Just a rough day with a few students. I got your message this morning. So far no luck with a Cynthia or a girl from Seattle area in general. But, I do have a few more people who might have some news." She rattled it off like how I answered my father on my chores during the summer.

"Thanks for jumping on that. I heard something about this young lady last night at the reception and wanted to see if there was any information about her. Nothing on a web search since I don't have a last name." I cleared my throat.

We chatted for just a minute about the Drake house and what the widow, Sarah wore for the reception. Just polite chatting. I nearly asked if she went out on a date last night, but wrangled my urge into submission.

"Julie, I gotta run. I'll let you know if I find out anything more. Bye." She hung up. I wasn't sure what just happened, but that wasn't the usual Porsche. I ran over the conversation, but I hadn't said very much. I would have to call her tomorrow.

When I walked home for lunch, I headed right for the mailboxes next to the clubhouse. This was the unofficial gathering spot for sharing and gathering news of the neighbors. Lanky Delores and short Beverly quickly joined me, but there was no sign of Nathan. *How did they know the instant I arrived?*

I'd hoped to wrangle out of Nathan who his Doctor friend was. Seems I would have to catch up to him later.

"Ladies, I need your help. Either of you know somebody from Pastor Tom's church? I'm specifically hoping to talk with the secretary but I need her to open up to me." I took a breath but they only glanced at one another. "I figure if I was introduced by a regular of the church she might talk more freely with me." I looked from one to the other.

Delores licked her lips. "Well, I know her. She used to attend my church before she took the job with Pastor Tom. We sang in the choir together."

"Do you think we could ... she would meet with us. I would really like to ask some questions." Delores was already shaking her head no.

"I know she would never talk openly if you're there. I don't know if she'll discuss much with me since we haven't kept up."   She looked hard at me.   "How important is this?"

"I found out a few things about Pastor Tom at his funeral reception last night..."

"Hold the phone young lady!   You went to the reception?" Delores said with a stern tone.

"Did anybody connect you with that article?" Beverly questioned.

"Nobody recognized me, I had a disguise."   I smiled bright.

"You are just lucky little miss that somebody didn't know who you were and call the police or something." Delores at her core was the voice of warning...for pretty much everything.

"I served hor d'oeuvres and listened to people gossip. I wasn't doing anything wrong."   I counted to ten and I suspect Delores did as well.

Beverly got the conversation back on track. "What is it you need with the church secretary?"

"I need to confirm there were marital problems and Sarah was on the verge of leaving him. I also need to know if she remembers a girl attending named Cynthia what happened in that situation."   Delores had started taking notes and looked up when I stopped.

"Well, there's also a rumor..." I coughed. "Does she know anything about Pastor Tom and a monthly swingers group." Delores's eyes narrowed accusingly and her mouth pursed. Beverly chuckled.

"Young lady, I'll have lunch with Meredith and bring up Pastor Drake. You'll see that you're wrong about the Good Pastor and these rumors are vicious lies."

"How soon can you talk with her?" I slapped my hand over my mouth. That slipped out. She turned and walked away. I hope this hadn't broken the harmony of our little community. I turned to Beverly with a pleading look.

"Don't worry just yet. She may have to see some of her own idols brought tumbling down, but she can't blame you for what the man was or did." She shrugged. "See you tonight." I checked my watch, I needed to grab a bite and get back to work.

Tonight was pinochle night in the clubhouse. I was okay at the card game but needed more practice anyway and it brought a good crowd. We usually had four tables of four playing and Nathan was a regular.

I managed to make a quick hard Italian Salami and Swiss sandwich to go. I ate as I walked back to work. The rest of the afternoon went by with routine tasks. My father called asking how it went with the lawyer and for once we didn't argue and I was glad he phoned.

It was Thursday night and I was exhausted, mentally and emotionally. I opted out of Pinochle at the clubhouse and considered the movies I could watch instead. I wanted something to take my mind off the death, and I didn't feel up to a crowd or noise like at

Pinochle night. I figured I could find a science fiction, fantasy, or vampire movie along with a bucket of fresh popped popcorn slathered in real butter and enjoy a calm evening. I was going to be a couch potato and just relax. I would catch up to Nathan tomorrow and ask about his doctor friend.

Unfortunately, a quiet evening was not for me. My family had left me alone too much this past week. As I walked up to my house, I saw my cousins Felicia and Loring standing on my front porch with the door open and the lights blazing. Felicia was in a fifties era retro-style dress in pink while Loring wore a band tour t-shirt and jeans and although I couldn't see Aunt Regina and Uncle Lars, I knew they were inside. My aunt was enveloped in her favorite soft blue color palate that accentuated her olive complexion. My uncle wore his relaxed denim jeans and a sweatshirt.

My aunt and uncle have keys as my back-up, so they surprise me sometimes for family night. I smiled at the thought of Aunt Regina's homemade food while simultaneously groaning inside at the chaos the night promised. *Wonder what we were having?*

Rather than enter through the garage, I walked to the front door to greet my cousins. Loring gave me a playful punch on the arm. We were still on the porch and I was already getting abuse.

"How's my cousin holding up after breaking Brandon's heart?" I couldn't tell if he was serious or not.

"Is he that broken up?" I didn't want to hurt him, but I hoped he would realize how insensitive he had been.

"Well, he'll be okay but he's feeling a bit lost. You guys have known each other for so long, I don't think he knows how to move on or ask a girl out." He put his arm around me. "But, I took him out to party to get snockered and start the healing." This was not what I wanted to hear.

"Well, I hope he finds more healing than from juvenile escapist methods."

Loring stuck his tongue out at me. "This is why I pulled your hair when we were younger, you always treated me like a Neanderthal."

"I may have, but if you're honest you went out of your way to be a chauvinist just to make me mad." Oh, the joys of family. Having no brothers or sisters Felicia and Loring became substitute siblings for me.

He smiled brightly. "That's one perspective." He always knew how to send my blood pressure soaring and he delighted in doing it. We related best in adversarial roles, nothing mushy for us.

I heard a voice that was out of place and slowly turned to see Mason in the kitchen with my aunt. Aunt Regina looked at me and exclaimed, "We met your new neighbor when he questioned us walking into your house. I decided he needed a good home cooked meal." Mason smiled brightly from behind her. Was that an apron he had on? It had a photo of a Sheltie dog and the words "Dog hair adds flavor." I don't think that was from Aunt Regina or uncle Lars. I wanted to run up to my room and lock myself in. How did Mason get invited into my house, my sanctuary?

I was speechless.

Aunt Regina noticed, frowned at me and waved Felicia into motion. Felicia put a glass of Rothchild Bordeaux wine in my hand. It was cheap, but even a cheap Rothchild is good. I think I may have gulped it because Loring looked between Mason and me holding an empty wine glass and chuckled wickedly.

Uncle Lars came to my rescue, gave me a big hug, kissed my forehead, led me to my own couch and sat me down. There was cheese and crackers on the coffee table. Loring was quizzing Mason on what he did for a living while I thought I would hyperventilate. So much for a nice quiet evening to forget everything, take a mental vacation with that vampire movie. I started in on my second glass of wine when my sweet uncle took the glass and handed me some cheese on a cracker.

"Mon petite, slow down. We're here for you. Don't worry yourself about everything from this week." He motioned for me to eat some cheese. "We want to cheer you, not stress you." He smiled and lowered his voice so only I could hear him. "Brandon was an idiot. He never understood you, your dreams, nor your drive to make them a reality. You two didn't fit, he didn't fit your jeux de vivre." He got up to help with dinner.

Did I say how I love my aunt and uncle? Uncle Lars runs an art gallery in Manitou Springs, the funky touristy town is a touch hippy and new age, but fun. It snuggles up against the mountain and became known as a health spot in the eighteen hundreds for its natural mineral springs that the native Ute Indians had long imbibed. The name Manitou was Algonquian the term for a spirit controlling nature, and Springs because of the mineral springs. It is seamlessly adjacent to Colorado Springs. Lars sells his own paintings and a few other artists' work. Regina plays viola for the Colorado Springs Symphony when she isn't working in the gallery or giving music lessons.

I just had to breathe and remember I wasn't the instigator in inviting Mason over. Porsche would understand, she knew my family. I heard a bark and Mason's Sheltie ran over to me. I began petting Roulette and she attempted to climb into my lap. I let her rest her front paws on my lap, but she was too big to be a lapdog. I leaned back against the couch and absently stroked the friendly dog. If I slowed down she nuzzled my hand.

I was letting the week wash over me while cooks in the kitchen fussed, dishes were being set at the table, more wine was being opened, even a CD began playing on my stereo, while I stared into Roulette's eyes and kept petting her.

My week whirled through my mind. I felt the sorrow of seeing a person dead and the blow to my relationship with Brandon, my fear of the police accusing me, the pressure of my father's wishes, the fear of losing my resort manager-in-training position. Each item came to mind and I looked at it while I pet the dog. Before I knew it she was in my lap and I knew my life would never quite be the same again and I had to find peace with the change, the loss of innocence about the ugly world around me.

The rest of the evening was a blur of chicken asparagus crepes and almond cake with more wine. I had to tell the whole story to them of Pastor Tom, the police questioning me at work, my stint as a server at the funeral reception for the caterer, and what I had found so far. I left out the potential swingers.

When I talked about listening in at the reception, Aunt Regina shook her head in disapproval. I don't think it was amazement but rather "when will she ever learn to leave well enough alone" on her face. Uncle Lars hid a smile while Felicia was upset I hadn't asked her to help, which got a deeper frown from Regina. Loring had the look of amazement. I think I surprised him I had the guts to do it. Mason was hard to read. He appeared to be watching my family's reactions more than having his own opinion.

Everyone decided that watching one of the movies was a great idea. Movie night with this gang is an interactive event. Popcorn may be tossed at the screen, there are boos or cheers. Yes, I enjoy the heckling antics too. I'm the one who usually is yelling "don't go in there...don't do it" to the actors. If I really want to focus on a movie I don't watch it with them.

We picked the science fiction movie because it had the most heckling potential and I experienced a moment of panic when everybody was getting seated and there was just enough room to squeeze in between Mason and Felicia.

I grabbed a chair from the dinner table and moved it into view of the large screen TV that usually stayed hidden in an armoire. Mason raised his eyebrows at my move.

I admit it, I had fun and felt much better by the time goodbyes were said. Mason walked out with my family, Roulette by his side, but doubled back when their cars were down the road. Roulette obediently stayed where he had commanded and watched.

"I just wanted to say how much fun I had. I hope my being invited by your Aunt didn't cause any problems." He had walked up the few steps and faced me on the porch. I moved closer to the door for a quick escape.

"I'm tired and a bit stressed, coming home to the 'wild bunch' was a bit overwhelming. It's nothing personal. I'd just planned on spending the night watching movies alone and found that wasn't happening. But, I guess it was what I needed." I smiled a reserved smile, not encouraging but neighborly.

"You know, as your neighbor, and I hope as a friend, you don't have to watch movies alone unless you prefer. I'm always up for a movie, quiet or rowdy." He handed me a slip of paper. "There's my cell phone number and email. Just give me a call."

His smile made his eyes appear full of mischief. He moved close to me before I could bolt he whispered, "Your listening in at the reception was something I would've done. Maybe we're more alike than you think." His breath hot on my cheek and his wavy hair brushing my lips. I swallowed. My heart was hammering. Maybe I should mention Porsche about now because she had dibs on him. Besides, I was a Bourne girl.

He kissed my cheek and lingered over it as if he was considering more. I was a statue, unable to move, rooted in place, not daring to breathe.

Then he turned and jogged across the street to a dancing Roulette and I darted inside like a frightened rabbit ducking in my hole. I didn't encourage him. I didn't invite him to dinner and a movie, that was all my aunt. Porsche would understand, right?

Chapter Twelve

Friday mornings I usually slept in since I have the day off, but I had to go into the office to check on an event. It was only a few hours and then I did the normal things like grocery shopping and errands. I got back to Resort Shadows in the afternoon and strolled out to the mailboxes, walking past Nathan's unit. I found Nathan leaning against the tree that shades his porch.

"I was wondering when you were going to get by to see me. You stood me up last night for a party with that new guy." He placed his hand over his heart. "I'm devastated. After everything we've meant to each other." He couldn't keep his smile from breaking out. His white hair was tied in a ponytail again today.

"You'll always be in my heart. But, my aunt was the instigator with my neighbor, not me." That was still my story and I was completely sticking to it.

"So what's up? I hear you gave Delores an assignment she isn't happy about."

I explained about the funeral reception and trying to find the church secretary to see if some of the overheard conversations were true.

"I really want to find out more about this Cynthia from Seattle and if Pastor Tom's wife was close to leaving him. Delores knows the secretary so she is going to talk to her. Mostly I think she wants to prove Pastor Tom isn't involved in everything I have found." He studied me for several breaths.

"What are you planning on doing with all this information?"

"It's looking like I'm the prime suspect. Did you read the newspaper article?" He nodded. "The police detective who grilled made it clear he thinks I killed the Pastor. I want to hand them what I've found and provide others with motive to kill Drake." He nodded again. I took that as a sign to continue.

"I'd like to find out more about the swingers and see if that leads to somebody that would've killed him." Nathan continued to look at me. I shifted my weight.

"That's a dead-end, dear. The doctor who mentioned it never accepted the invitation, so he only knows Drake in the group. I can call him and ask about the Padre's murder, see if he has anything to add. There's a slim chance he knows something, although I doubt it. I'll call if I find anything." He didn't move.

"Something bothering you?" I ventured.

Nathan's eyes scrunched. "I'd rather keep your name from any more connection to this. You've been exposed enough with that article, and let's not forget that there is a killer out there who's probably happy to have you under suspicion."

Well, he had a point there. I didn't want to be connected with this incident any more than necessary and I didn't want to draw the killer's attention either.

"Were you the only person working that event that day?"

"No, we were providing a buffet for lunch so we had the food preparers and servers helping to set the food and tables up. Why?"

"I know you didn't kill the padre, but what about the other employees?" I hadn't considered the resort staff, I immediately considered them as being outside the drama taking place. But it made sense that the staff might know something, seen something, or maybe had the opportunity to strike during the few minutes available. Could Anete have seen something?

"I'll start looking into the staff that worked that day. Thanks."

I strolled home and I tried to do some cleaning. I just felt at odds wanting to do something more about the murder. I was stuck waiting on Delores to talk to the church secretary and Nathan to ask around, but I wanted to do something.

I gave up and went back to my office with the sole idea of compiling who worked the day of Pastor Tom's murder in addition to the luncheon attendance list that disappeared. I thought I could piece together a list from my plans and notes on the events along with emails, but I just didn't have a complete picture.

I started a file on everything I had found so far. I added the printouts from the internet I had brought from home on Sarah Drake, Robert Crandel, and David Babcock. The big mysteries were Seattle Cynthia and any swingers group.

I would have to wait until Sunday to talk with Claudia and look at the human resources files since she kept them all locked up. I knew Anete and Brad were there. That left the rest of today and Saturday waiting. Saturday there weren't any events or even hotel activities for me to oversee, so I had the day free. At least I felt I was doing something now, not pacing at home waiting to be the police's quick resolution and scapegoat on this hot potato of a case.

I sat back in my rickety office chair. It was surprising how quiet the office area was with little to no foot traffic. The hair on the back of my neck was prickling at the sound of someone approaching. It occurred to me that a killer was still free and the memory of my unlocked office door the other morning flashed in my mind. The footsteps stopped and silence stretched. I reached for the phone, but before I could lift the receiver...

"There you are. I've been looking everywhere." A man's voice tinged with impatience rang out, seemingly bouncing off the hallway walls. I judged him right outside my door.

"Come on, I ducked into a bathroom and then you were gone." A huff punctuated the woman's strident peel. I could hear them walk away, but I swear I could hear another set of steps, much slower and hard to determine direction.

The hair on my arms was electrified. I tiptoed to my doorway and glanced around the hallway. Nothing. Not. A. Soul. I inhaled deeply and blew it out. *Get a grip, don't start imagining a Boogie man around every corner.*

Just for the sake of doing something to focus on, I tried an internet search on Swingers, although I expected very little or nothing. My mouth hung open to find two swingers sites for the Colorado Springs area. Minimal details on the opening pages because you had to join what looked like a dating site.

I was alone in the administration area and yet I was embarrassed to be on these sites. I did find a site that explained the lifestyle. It claimed Swinging may have started in the fifties among the military. Considering Colorado Springs had several military bases and installations, maybe the presence of the websites wasn't so amazing after all.

I didn't want to join those sites just to ask questions ... and I'd be horrified if I knew anybody. Some things are better left unknown. I continued on and found the local Independent paper had done an article about swingers in the area. Apparently, the lifestyle is so counter to the conservative religious bent in town that it made it newsworthy. The idea struck me that maybe I could ask the reporter for a contact to do my own investigation.

I found the reporter and her contact information. I was about to send an email from my personal account but realized my name was too recognizable from that blasted paper article fingering me as a killer. I created a new email account with a different name associated. I went with Rhapsody at a free email site after Gershwin's Rhapsody in Blue, one of my favorite clarinet pieces and I made Rhapsody Blue the name on the account too.

I sent the email from the new account and wrote I was interested in doing some research on the swingers in the area for a book and did she have any contacts she could share. I put the new email login information into the file I was gathering so I wouldn't forget completely about it. I knew I would forget this new account because it's only for one purpose. It was likely a long shot it would work, but I was hopeful that would provide something.

I stared at my framed poster of Castagnola Lake Lugano Resort in Switzerland hanging over my computer and thought about how much I had gathered so far. It was all circumstantial, nothing that would convince the police to look at another person seriously. Since I wasn't the killer, there was a murderer out there who didn't want to pay for the crime. I thought of my unlocked door and the footsteps in the hall a moment ago and a shiver slithered up my spine.

And what about the crime, stabbed through the heart? Okay, the ice sculpture was a weapon of opportunity. I heard that from the cops shows I watched. But stabbing directly into the heart with such thrust, well that was just vicious, full of rage. Pastor Tom was doubled over in pain when I left him and I'd be surprised if he had moved far from the spot. He probably couldn't have defended himself much since I had nearly incapacitated him in addition to his drunken state. Perhaps a person wouldn't have needed much strength, just a good shove and the element of surprise. Not for the first time, I wondered if Anete had seen somebody...or could she have... No! No, not Anete.

Whoever the killer was, he or she had slipped into the room, somehow shoved or dislodged the ice sculpture, then likely shoved Drake back onto the sword end, and ran out all within a few short minutes. That was decisive action, and I felt somebody had waited for the opportunity and did not hesitate when the chance presented itself. That was a cold calculating killer.

I was tense and jumpy just thinking about such a person lurking. *Shake it off girl.* I focused and began to organize the information on those involved so it was easier to see what I had, or didn't have.

I created a spreadsheet with the columns for motive, means, alibi, and down the left side the names of everybody I was considering. Everybody but "staff" had a motive but were present at the event so they the opportunity to slip into the room unobserved.

Of course, I had no idea about the family of Seattle Cynthia since I didn't even know the last name, but I listed them anyway. Maybe I should add a general "jealous person" until I discovered more details on the young women he was reputed as taking on as projects, besides the potential of jealousy if a swinger's club was involved.

This little exercise showed me I definitely needed more information all the way around. I could talk to the staff who worked the event and ask if they knew where the luncheon attendees had been during the buffet preparations. It occurred to me that some of the staff at the luncheon also worked other wait-staff jobs at the restaurants. I phoned the restaurants and the second one had Anete working today.

I printed out my table of suspects, shut down the computer and locked up with my file in hand. I strolled through the shops complex to one of the hotel restaurants. Anete, the young lady who discovered Pastor Tom à la shish kabob, was working the lunch rush in the airy solarium garden restaurant known for its enormous chandelier with rose and white crystal droplets suspended from the soaring solarium ceiling.

I asked to be seated where Anete could wait on me. I'd have to shell out some money for lunch to talk to her, But I felt this was the easiest way. The sunshine cascading down through the glass ceiling onto the white linen covered tables lifted my spirits.

"Miss Julienne, it's nice to see you again." She had given me only a few minutes to look at the menu before appearing, perfectly timed.

"The Shrimp Salad Louis please. But, I have a question first."

"What would you like to know? Everything is on the menu, but I can provide more information on listed items." Her accent was clearly European, but hard to place even though I knew her country of origin.

"I need to know about the other day, was there anything unusual that happened? Did you see anybody else in the banquet room? Anyone acting oddly?"

She glanced around and licked her lips and her eyes grew large. "I don't know ma'am. It was a shock."

"Did Pastor Drake ever say or do anything inappropriate? Take liberties with you?" I hated to even ask, but I had to.

"If you are asking what I think you are, no. Nothing like that. I saw nobody else in the room."

"Did you notice anything that was out of the ordinary?"

"I don't like to say. I don't want to be in trouble for complaining."

"Don't worry, just tell me." I leaned forward.

"Somebody brought their phone with them and took a call while we were setting up the banquet table."

"Well, that's against the rules. Was that the only thing different you noticed?" She nodded. I was disappointed; a small infraction of the rules wasn't the information I was hoping for.   "Who brought their phone and took the call?"

She swallowed and looked around again. "Brad, the new guy."

I would mention it to him next time I saw him, but otherwise, this talk was a bust. Unless there was an indication that Anete was directly involved, I doubted she knew anything worthwhile.

The Shrimp Salad Louis was fantastic, so the time wasn't completely a waste.

Chapter Thirteen

I knew Pastor Tom had some drinks, so he wasn't in any of the breakout sessions since they served only water or coffee. I figured Pastor Tom had ducked across the street to the small pub-themed bar and had a few drinks, so I planned on stopping there on my way home.

I stopped at the Gilded Hornet bar on my way home, my file tucked under my arm. It was a recreation of an old English Pub complete with Victorian English décor and classic pub food, the warm beer cheese and crackers were my weakness.

I knew only a few people who worked here. Luckily Ramone was behind the dark mahogany bar. There were already a few couples seated, but by evening it would be crowded for the sing-along with the piano player. It was a fun tradition at the Gilded Hornet that drew regulars from town as well as hotel guests.

"Hola bella dama," Ramone called out when he saw me while continuing wiping down the high gloss bar top. He always made me feel special with his greeting. I suspected he was good at making most customers feel that way.

"Hola, guapo." That was the extent of my abilities with Spanish. I sat on a bar stool, placing the file on the bar.

"Wine or something a little stronger this afternoon? I keep telling you I make a fine Mojito that will relax you and make you feel warm all over." He could make drinks sound so sensual. Probably why he was one of the resort's best bartenders. That and his good looks made him very popular. Sometimes I wondered how many of the women came for the sing-along or just for Ramone's charm.

"Nothing to drink, I wanted to ask you about the other day. Was Pastor Tom in here? I could smell liquor on his breath and was wondering where he'd gotten the booze?"

He leaned over the bar a little, I met him halfway and he whispered to me. "He was in here for just a few minutes, he downed two bourbons, checked out the few people sitting around and left. I don't think he wanted to draw attention to himself, but I have to say he knocked those drinks back like an old pro. He seemed well acquainted with alcohol."

"Did you see anybody follow him outside, anything unusual?"

He chuckled. "The police already asked me this. They even asked if you were in here with him. I told them you were out of his league altogether."

"Thanks for standing up for me." I felt heat rush to my face with such high praise. "I know they think I'm a suspect, but it makes me mad. The guy assaulted me and they think I was propositioning him."

"I heard he got grabby with you. That tidbit has been going around. I'd have knocked his teeth out for you." The perpetual motion of his wiping the bar halted as he strangled the bar rag. The twinkling eyes flashed anger for a second, then it was gone and his usual flirtatious glint returned along with the scrubbing of the bar top. "Keep that in mind if anybody else manhandles you. We have to look out for each other." He winked.

He pointed at the file next to my elbow. "Taking work home? Doesn't Chad ever give you a break?"

"Oh, just some homework. Chad's a task master all right." I didn't want to sound ridiculous saying I was compiling information on the murder. I changed the subject.

"Tell me what you've heard. Did anybody have a reason to kill him that was in here or the convention center that day?" We were practically whispering in each other's ear.

"I hear all sorts of things. There are people who say he was a hypocrite, that he was a dog with younger ladies. I heard a couple of women just last night in here talking about his prowess and they each had a story to tell. They were toasting his stamina and how they would miss some monthly hook up. Some of these women were lookers too." He sprayed cleaning solution and kept wiping the bar as he whispered.

Here I was trying to find information on the elusive swingers group and they were here last night and Ramone had served them.

"Did you get any phone numbers, names?" I winked. He looked down and even in the subdued lighting I think his ears turned red. Could Ramone be all talk and swagger only?

"No, no. Nothing like that." He still didn't look up.

"How about names? Did they pay with a card?" I had my fingers and toes crossed.

"No, cash. But if you are thinking one of them may have been jealous and killed him, no. I can tell you it wasn't them. They were telling each other intimate details with no passion of attachment." Really? I guess I'm not made that way. I'm the proverbial one-man-woman and I find it hard to comprehend that mindset.

"Some people are detached and it is just a physical act." I must have raised an eyebrow for he quickly added, "Not me, I've heard some people are this way." A response that was negative towards the male gender jumped into my mind and I pushed it aside. I was not the best at relationships so I couldn't slam all men.

"If not them, how about their husbands? These women were married weren't they?" He avoided my eyes again and his compulsive polishing of the bar top became more vigorous. "They're not your usual couples I think. They ... I mean ..." I decided to help him out.

"They're swingers?   Wife swappers?   Is that what you're trying to tell me?"

He stopped his polishing and stared at me.   "Yes, that's exactly what I'm saying. And from what I heard each of them have been married for a long time, but they also have been swapping for a long time. They'd talk about times years back. They aren't new to it, so I think their husbands aren't beginners either."

He glanced around before continuing.   "If any of them were jealous types they wouldn't have lasted so long." How could a bartender possibly tell all that? I take that back. I'd known Ramone to look at a couple and tell how serious they were, how close to proposing the guy was and whether she would marry him. He could read people.   Co-workers would bet him on friends that came in, believing they had an inside track. Didn't matter, I hear he hadn't been wrong about a couple yet. But still, I wasn't ready to give up on the swingers angle, not yet.

"What about the gossip of Pastor Tom with girls, did you get any names?"

"In the last several days there's been all kinds of talk. Some of it's just tearing him down because he was well known and some seemed to actually know him. A few mentioned him with girls but never said any names. Like they were nobody."

He clenched his fist holding the bar rag. " I didn't sense anybody really cared about the girls, just the scandal of the Pastor misusing them. I think of my little sister and it makes me mad." The last words were more a growl and the fist holding the bar rag was a chokehold and the lethal look in his eyes.

It made me mad too, but if I had a young sister I would no doubt be more upset. Nameless, faceless girls may have been preyed upon by an authority figure and nobody cared about them, just the sensational story of the guy who was low enough to use them. I was more determined to find out if there was any truth to the rumors. The girls deserved justice.

"You're a good brother, Ramone. It makes me mad too. Will you keep your ears open, maybe ask a few people quietly if they know the names of any of these poor girls? Maybe we can get them a slice of justice that they deserve." His jaw clenched a few times.

"I'll do my best to find out. I'll do it for all my sisters." I didn't know how many sisters he had, but I hoped to put names to any faceless victims.

Ramone promised to phone my office if he found anything. I left to walk home to Resort Shadows with my file folder tucked under my arm.

Chapter Fourteen

The second Friday of each month was "social night" at the clubhouse. I figured it was just what I needed after a day of contemplating the dark mind that would kill or prey on impressionable young people. I decided I might even have a drink. I am cautious drinking around Beverly and Delores, they got me drunk last year before I even knew what happened. Don't let those grandmotherly ladies fool you, they can handle their liquor.

I had picked up a few things in the afternoon with the social hour in mind. On my way out my door, I grabbed the bucket of margaritas. I had already poured the tequila in the bucket mix and popped into the freezer a few hours ago so it was now slushy. That and the cheese and cracker tray was my contribution.

I placed everything on the porch and grabbed my sweater coat since it was cooler in the evenings. It was a lovely dusk this autumn day. I slung the bucket of margaritas handle onto one arm and hoisted the cheese tray with the cracker box lying on top. I carefully descended my three front steps watching my footing and ran right into Mason.

"Oh, so sorry. I didn't mean to run into you." I made the mistake of looking up into his eyes. I marveled at his long lush eyelashes. His eyes were direct and smoldering. I never understood that word until now. But, smoldering was the only word for the restrained fire in his eyes.

"I did." His hair looked so enticing falling in soft waves around his face, his mouth was in a wolfish grin. I couldn't help but wonder at how different the photo of him gambling seemed from the flirtatious man before me. "May I help you?" He held out his hands. *Oh, what the hell.* I handed him the chilled bucket of margaritas.

"I hear there's a shindig in the club house, that where we're headed?"

"I'm sure not drinking all this by myself. It'll be gone in a few minutes with this gang." I couldn't avoid Mason since he lived smack dab across the street from me. He certainly wasn't avoiding me. I'd just have to make the best of it and tonight I was going to have a little fun. After all, I'd had a rough week. At least the bomb threat had been a fluke. I little frivolous enjoyment was definitely in order.

The clubhouse was not huge, but it held about thirty-five people comfortably and I had seen far more squeezed into the main level with the kitchen and lounge area. It had a hot tub downstairs with showers and a sauna. The upstairs had a pool table and a modest bar setup you had to stock if you wanted to use it. The clubhouse was comfortable and I was happy to see it used as a community gathering spot. The lounge area had a few more chairs setup around the couch and matching chairs, but it was filling up already.

Mason helped me set up my cheese tray and crackers and even got us both some margaritas before it was all consumed. There was wine, some homemade Sangria, and beer along with bottled water, pitchers of lemonade or punch. Food ran from a pasta bar with three different kinds of pastas and sauces, salads and some desserts.

I mingled and even played hostess and introduced Mason to some of the other homeowners. I was aware that he didn't wander far from my side. I told myself he didn't know the others well and after spending the evening with my family I was naturally an anchor for him. Yeah, that had to be it, because a General's son who played high stakes poker and photographed models would be shy around people he didn't know.

I dished up some angel hair pasta, drizzled pesto sauce over it, added some hand grated Parmesan, and threw in some sliced black olives. The margaritas were already drained empty. I was juggling my pasta plate and about to pour some Sangria when Mason took my glass and poured for me.

"I secured us a spot at that table over by the fireplace, I'll bring your wine over." I was quickly getting the impression that this social hour was becoming a date and I thought of Porsche with a pang of guilt. I had to face that he did just fine with people on his own, he didn't actually need me, and he was by my side because he wanted to stay close. It made me feel special and want to giggle like a schoolgirl. I kept any juvenile giggling strictly internal.

I'd have to keep things platonic, friends, and neighbors only. Besides, after the models I saw him with on the gossip websites, he probably thought of me as his sister more than a potential date. The attention was nice, but I had to keep from reading more into it than was likely there.

I enjoyed myself and Mason chatted with other neighbors. After a margarita and few Sangrias, I began to feel more comfortable, like we were just friends and he needed to warm up to this strange grouping of people that was Resort Shadows. I was standing across the room near the door to the patio and swimming pool between conversations.

"You two seem to have hit it off." Beverly snuck up and surprised me as I was watching Mason talk with J.R., one of the golfers in our little village. Her compact size was always dressed in perfectly matched outfits and jewelry. Tonight one tattoo on her upper arm was visible, the large butterfly, due to her butterscotch orange sleeveless blouse. "I hear he even met the family already."

"It's not like that. My aunt invited him to dinner before I even got home from work, so that wasn't me.

We're just neighbors and I'm introducing him around. Besides, he and my friend are dating."

"Your friend and Mason? You mean that professor friend of yours that's got as many commitment issues as a politician during election season?" Porsche wasn't afraid of commitment. She just never found a guy she wanted around for more than a month or two. Hmmm, why was I so worried about this mess, they may not date for long. But, I wasn't a Bond girl I reminded myself.

"Porsche's more his type I think," I stated.

"He knows his type better than you." She slowly shook her head. "I swear, you're blind sometimes girl."

"You always know how to bolster me and make me feel good." I lightly punched her in the arm. Time to change the subject "So, is Delores mad and avoiding me?" I hadn't seen her and usually she was anywhere there was alcohol to be had. Maybe that's why there was some wine still available.

"She's having dinner with that church secretary. I expect we'll hear how it went tomorrow if she can stand to tell us. I think she's in for a surprise." Beverly smiled like a Cheshire cat. "Don't worry. She'll get over it."

We chatted a little about the upcoming pinochle game night. The group was thinking of doing a championship match with playoffs over the next few game nights.

Mason joined us just as Beverly said, "You need work on your partner bidding if you want to make it into the playoffs."

"I play cards. But I've never heard of pinochle. Is it like Bridge?" I managed not to choke over the innocent look when he said he played cards. He was looking between Beverly and me with lighthearted interest.

"It isn't as thrilling as high stakes poker, but it has some strategy and a level of competition." Beverly glanced at me. "Julie's coming along in her playing the game, maybe she could teach you." Beverly beamed. She thought she was clever, but her move was so transparent I was uncomfortable. I shifted weight from one foot to the other.

"Porsche and I used to play. She could give you some lessons too." I was rather proud of myself slipping Porsche in like that. It must have worked because Mason tilted his head slightly and studied me. "I'll ask her about that." Beverly kicked my foot with the toe of her shoe. I barely managed to keep from yelping in surprise. She was sly, that little tattooed dynamo.

"Mason, I saw you chatting with J.R. about golf. Do you play much?" *Oh good, we were moving to safer ground.*

"I took lessons last year when I was shooting a series of photos for a golf resort magazine. I haven't played much in the last several months with moving and all." He was still studying me as if he could read my thoughts if he watched my face long enough. *Was this what it was like to play poker with him?*   It was a bit unnerving. I took a gulp of my water I was holding.

"Resort Shadow's owners get a discount at the Resort golf club or general membership. It just so happens that Julie here could set you up with a membership."

I elbowed her slightly in her arm. She looked between Mason and me as we stared at each other.

"I think I'm going to claim my dishes and go home now." She proclaimed, planning to run out at this awkward time. I quickly hugged her before she escaped and whispered, "I'll get even for that missy."

"I just might be interested in a golf membership. I could come by your office and discuss the details with you." He was looking deep into my eyes with a question in his.

"I'd be happy to go over the different levels of membership we provide and see what would be right for you. But I'm calling it a night." *Keep it friends, platonic, neighbors.* He wasn't that easily left behind, though. He helped me gather up my remaining cheese and crackers then walked with me on the pathway past the tennis court and swimming pool. There was a light breeze bringing the crisp earthen smells of fallen leaves laced with a trace of moisture and a fireplace. I was glad I brought my sweater coat.

"Have you found out much more in your search for suspects?"

"Delores had dinner tonight with the church secretary to see if she could clear Tom's name from the gossip I heard. Tomorrow I hope to hear how that went. I've started a file to keep everything organized." I took a few breaths as I considered how much to share.

I briefly mentioned the swinger possibility that Nathan had brought to light. I went for an "oh by the way" tone since the topic had the potential to embarrass me and I didn't want that right now.

"I made an inquiry into the Independent paper about an article they did on Swingers to see if I can get a contact to interview for a book I claimed to be writing." It had all tumbled out, maybe because it was not personal talk and I wanted to keep him at a distance. It felt good just to have somebody to go over everything.

"You're thinking this Swinger group has potential of leading somewhere?" His voice was neutral, smooth as velvet. I didn't dare look at him in the moonlight. I was already too aware of his presence next to me, the whiffs of his spicy cologne were near intoxicating.

Oh hell, it was hard to not give into just wanting that steamy fling Porsche had been encouraging. But, I'd never been the type to have a fling. I was the true blue gal who was faithful and devoted to a fault. I would never be one of those fabled "friends with benefits" because my feelings got involved no matter what I tried to tell myself.

It hurt deeply to lose my Mom at the age of ten. I know Aunt Regina has talked to me over the years, concerned I hadn't dealt well with my mother's death and sabotaged relationships as a result. After getting my heart broke so often in high school maybe that was why I dated Brandon, he had been around the family since my childhood, had even known my mother, he was permanent feeling. Mason Sheridan had "heartbreak" and "temporary" written all over his muscular body. *Gulp.*

"Seems to me that the entire swinger's setup is a jealous murder waiting to happen. The swingers seem like a perfect situation for the kind of passion that would make somebody stab a guy through the heart." The words continued to tumble out even with my mind screaming to just shut up.

"I agree, it goes against my sense of a devoted couple. I've always been old fashioned in wanting a long-term marriage like my parents have. Loving, devoted, tender, monogamous, and loyal. I agree it's a setup for murder, I know I'd want to kill a man who touched my love." That was...unexpected. I think my mouth was hanging open. So much for the neutral topic, my heart skipped a beat...or five. His voice had stayed conversational, but he could've been whispering in my ear for how intimate it felt. I had to change the topic because his words were getting to me. Making me forget he was a heartbreaker or entertain the ridiculous fantasy that he'd stick around.

"Then there is Seattle Cynthia, as I call her." It was the only topic rolling around in my head to grab hold of and change the subject. "As far as I can tell, she was going to Drake's church and was one of his "special projects." That's what one of the people at the funeral reception called the girl's he took an interest in, his special projects. Somebody mentioned she returned home to Seattle and committed suicide. I keep thinking that the family would want justice. But I don't know the last name to follow up on it." I was rambling now. *Yep, I was cool and collected.*

We were nearing our homes and I was fighting with the desire for this companionable chatting to continue and yet wanting a locked door between Mason and myself. This was a new form of torture for me and I don't think I was handling it well. Not that, you understand, anything would happen, 'cause it's not like that. Sure, he seemed like a gentleman now, but who knows when dealing with a playboy type.

"Would you join me in walking Roulette. I'd like to discuss Seattle Cynthia more."

"Okay, I'll put my stuff away and be right back." I hated it when my mouth speaks without permission. There lies danger. It was like I was watching myself in a horror movie and I'm yelling at myself to not open that door and then I see myself do it anyway. When would I listen? I put my utensils in the sink and left over cheese from the tray into the fridge.

Mason had Roulette on a leash waiting on the sidewalk under a street lamp and a sickle-moon observing overhead. Roulette wore a reflective harness so she would be visible to cars. A little voice inside me whispered that a man who took such care of his dog had some good qualities. I mentally told that voice to keep its opinion to itself. *Sheesh.*

"So, we don't know Seattle Cynthia's last name." He picked up the conversation and we walked away from Resort Shadows. The breeze smelled of autumn with its promise of moisture on its way. I took a deep breath, inhaling the rich colors of autumn. Trees sighing and leaves twirling in their breath serenaded us along the way.

"Something tells me that this poor girl needs justice and that her family's heartbroken. That would create the rage to stab somebody in the heart." I envisioned Pastor Tom's lifeless eyes staring and shivered.

"I know what you told your family the other night, but sometimes talking about it can ease your mind. What happened when you were alone with him?" I couldn't look at him, and the last thing I wanted to share was the manhandling. Silence stretched between us, but he was clearly waiting. I gulped in a few more deep breaths and clenched my fists.

"There isn't much to tell, it happened so fast. I was checking the last preparations on the buffet table before the breakout sessions would end and the lunch begin." I stopped walking as I relived it. "I remember telling Brad to go get the crab claw cracker tools....Suddenly a hand grabbed my butt, rough."

I took another deep breath and found it was a little ragged. I was trying to be detached as I related what happened, but it wasn't working. "I yelled at him and tried to leave, he...grabbed my arm and pulled me to him. It left bruises.... I kneed him as hard as I could and left." A tear slid down my cheek. I didn't want to share that moment, I wanted to push it far away like it never happened. "He was doubled over holding his privates when I left and called resort security." I fought any more tears forming.

Roulette was sitting patiently waiting for us to move forward again. It occurred to me she must have had obedience training.

"You did nothing wrong. His actions were inexcusable and you did the right thing to get away. Don't doubt that for a minute." He took a finger and nudged my chin up so I looked him in the eyes. "Have you had any nightmares?"

Couldn't he just leave this alone?

"Sure, the whole thing was terrible. The next time I saw him he was so lifeless. That's a nightmare in itself." I whispered.

"You had a trauma and nightmares are common." He wiped a tear and smoothed a strand of hair behind my ear. "I'm always here to talk."

"I feel a little foolish. I mean, other women've gone through worse, I was lucky."

"You were very lucky. That doesn't mean it wasn't traumatic. Everybody deals with it differently and I'm just offering to be a shoulder to cry on or an ear to listen if you need it." Roulette saved the day by whining. She needed to relieve herself.

We started walking again and the conversation turned to life at Resort Shadows. Thank heavens! Between wrestling to keep my thoughts of Mason neighborly and revisiting Pastor Ted's rough hands on me, my emotions were close to the surface. I didn't know how well I would do if he wrapped his strong arms around me for comfort. Probably blubber like a baby and embarrass myself.

Roulette indicated she was done with her business and we turned back toward home.

"So your father is a general, was that hard growing up?"

"Growing up with a career oriented officer meant a lot of sacrifices for the family. My mother and I didn't see him much, and when we did we played the role of the perfect family at functions." He rubbed the back of his neck with a hand. "I was the artistic kid who wanted to study in Paris and paint, he wanted a son to follow him in the military. So, I did my stint in the service and got out, something I don't think he'll ever quite forgive me for doing."

I was surprised. Maybe we did have more in common than I thought. Both our parents disapproved of our choices for our future.

"My mother died of breast cancer when I was young, so my dad raised me along with Uncle Lars and Aunt

Regina. I saw plenty of him, that wasn't the problem. But we don't agree on my life direction either. My dad only wants me to get married and give him grandkids. By this time in my life I was to have married somebody rich and be on baby number two or three." We were now at our homes and the time together was about to end. Now to face the age old awkward good night.

"Julie, did you lock your door?"

I looked up and found my front door wide open.

Chapter Fifteen

Mason glared at the open door. He took something out of an inside jacket pocket and I heard a metal "snap". He was now wielding a retractable baton like the police might carry. I was surprised, yet oddly comforted that he had it handy.

"Roulette, attention." Roulette changed from a fluffy Sheltie to an alert scout, sniffing the air and ears up. If it were possible for the little dog to become a German Shepard, she would have. Her eyes scanned and searched the area.

"It might be best if you stay close to me, we don't know if there may be somebody outside lurking. I want you to stay just behind me." He looked me in the eyes to make sure I understood. I swallowed and nodded. I couldn't manage words at this point. Stabbings, bomb threats, and now somebody in my home, my safe retreat. *Would I ever sleep again?*

He started forward with Roulette and I followed a step or two behind, trying not to step on his heels. I watched Roulette for any sign that she sensed anything.

We moved up the three porch steps and the fully aware Sheltie paused at the threshold, sniffed the ground and then the air again and growled very low. Once inside, Roulette took the lead and ran up the stairs to the bedrooms, directly to the master bedroom. If it weren't for the front door standing wide open I would've suspected this was some sort of rehearsed ploy to seduce, but Mason and Roulette were all business.

The light was on in my room, which I know was wrong. Didn't burglars prefer to work in the dark rather than advertise? We walked in and there was a sheet of paper on my bed with extra large computer print declaring, "Back off before you get hurt." I could read it from the doorway. The note was exactly where I had sat my file with research on suspects.

I think Mason growled as he rotated the baton with an impressive roll of his wrist. He was full of surprises and I had no qualms staying close to him.

We searched the rest of my home and found my back door open too. It left me jumping at every breath or movement.

"Police?" Mason asked me.

I rubbed my temples, "I guess I better." Suddenly I was in his embrace breathing deeply of his cologne. He stroked my hair and I felt him kiss my temple. "Your Aunt and Uncle will want to know. Maybe you can stay with them tonight." The past week's stress finally caught up and I began to tremble. His embrace was my stability for a few brief moments.

I reluctantly broke free of the oasis his arms provided and phoned the police. Since I said there was no immediate danger it took forty-five minutes before they arrived. The city had suffered cuts to police and fire budgets and this was more and more the norm. Aunt Regina and Uncle Lars drove over before the police arrived. Mason's baton had disappeared before either my relatives or the police arrived and Roulette was a sweet fluffy dog waiting patiently.

"I'm calling you father, he will want to know." Uncle Lars had declared after removing his coat.

"Julienne, is that what you want right now?" Mason ignored Uncle Lars' arched eyebrow and open mouth.

There was no way to avoid telling dad for long. I nodded and Uncle Lars called dad. I smiled at Mason and mouthed *"Thanks."*

Between the two men over the phone, they decided that Dad didn't have to jump on the next flight, I was in good hands with local family. The men deciding things grated on my already frayed nerves, but I didn't want an argument either. *Let it go.*

The police finally pulled up and searched the house and the grounds before taking statements. The note was taken away so I didn't need to see it again. A few neighbors had gathered and Nathan handled letting them all know I was fine. This would be the talk of Resorts Shadows for the next few weeks. The police finally left and I felt utterly exhausted.

It was approaching midnight and I was so glad that I could sleep in tomorrow, but I was battling a slight panic of being alone after my sanctuary had been invaded. The police said my back door had been tampered leaving scratches around the lock.

"Mason, thank you so much for everything." I bent down and scratched Roulette's ears, "Thanks, Roulette, you were awesome." She licked my hand.

Aunt Regina moved to go upstairs and I knew she was going to pack an overnight bag and expected me to stay at their house.

"Guys, I'm staying here tonight." Aunt Regina stopped on the stairs and turned to look at me. Mason's eyebrows were raised and Uncle Lars' brows furrowed into a scowl.

"You can't stay here tonight for goodness sake." Aunt Regina's hands went to her hips.

"If I don't stay here tonight and face it, it will only get harder. I'm scared, but this is my home and I'm staying." Even if I didn't get any sleep, I needed to be in my house to reclaim it.

Aunt Regina came down the stairs and the three of them surrounded me and looked from one to the other.

"I promised your father, young lady." Uncle Lars' used the same tone I heard him use on my cousins over the years.

"I can stay here and sleep on the couch." Mason held up his hand. "I promise not to disturb you, but if not inside the house I'll be sleeping on your porch.

You aren't staying here alone tonight." His jaws were set even though his eyes were focused on watching every blink I made. There was no smoldering in those eyes now, just determination.

I caught the look that shot between my Aunt and Uncle. "We'd certainly feel better if you're here to ensure her safety." Regina purred at Mason.

I had to admit, if he were within yelling distance, I would feel better.

"I have a guest bedroom you and Roulette are welcome to use."

"Give me a few minutes to gather an overnight bag and I'll be right back before Regina and Lars leave." He turned and told Roulette to stay then jogged out the door.

"Are you sure you want to stay here? You know you're always welcome at Chez LaMere." Uncle Lars put a protective arm around me.

"I'm sure. Besides, I won't sleep any better staying elsewhere, worrying if they'll come back and do damage. Having Mason here will help me feel safer, and Roulette will give an early warning."

When Mason returned with a shaving kit and change of clothes, Regina and Lars left.

"I brought you something." His voice was weary, strained. He held out his hand and I took the offered item.

"What's this?" I was in a fog and couldn't seem to make sense of the label. Shock, or was I just emotionally overwhelmed?

"Pepper Spray."

"I don't know. I'm afraid I'll set it off and hit myself." Which was true. If it were possible, I'd likely manage it.

"I insist. I can't shadow you everywhere. I know I'll feel better if you have it with you at all times. You'll probably feel better having it too." His arms were folded across his chest. I suspected I was getting a glimpse of his stubborn side.

"Fine, fine." I slipped the fair sized canister into my purse.

He was a gentleman and kept a slight distance between us as I pointed to the spare bedroom that we had searched a few hours ago. He changed in the guest bathroom into pajama bottoms and another tee shirt. I got the impression he normally didn't wear a top to those bottoms. *Gulp.* He left his bedroom door open and Roulette lay down in the hallway just outside the door. I closed and locked my door.

I managed to go to sleep eventually from exhaustion, but I had nightmares through the night...until a muscular hero entered to chase away the shadows and fear.

Chapter Sixteen

My awareness returned slowly after a rather steamy dream with.... well you know. It seems my sub conscious liked the idea of a hot fling with the neighbor. Or more likely, I was under a lot of stress and being held and comforted in Mason's arms last night was putting a suggestion in my mind. I was clinging to that last explanation for all I was worth. Coffee and bacon smells broke through and I realized Mason must be in my kitchen, or possibly one of my family.

I searched my closet for a robe to slip on and finally found one in the back. This one was a light cotton with satin trimmed edges. Once I was properly wrapped up, I opened my bedroom door and peeked out. I glanced in the spare bedroom and saw the bed was made and I chalked that up to his being raised by a general. I heard whistling from downstairs. Today the tune was *"Here Come the Sun."*

I decided to quickly dress and brush my hair. I dressed in a sweatshirt advertising Seattle and baggy sweatpants. If I could've found a burlap sack I would've worn it. I swear. I braided my hair into a long single braid down my back and took my time down the stairs.

I stood just outside the open kitchen and stared as Mason was crumbling bacon into an egg mixture, whipped it, then poured it into a pie pan with a baked crust and slid it into the oven. The universe was simply being cruel at this point. The man could cook too. The old saying about "if it seems too good to be true, it probably is" was echoing through my head when he looked up and flashed a lazy smile and a lock of wavy hair fell forward caressing his cheek.

My breath caught at the sight and I fought the urge to smooth that curl back. He was dressed in a button down dress shirt tucked into his dark blue jeans and barefoot. *Okay. Okay, I surrender.* Maybe...just maybe, he's my type after all. Sheesh. But where did that leave Brandon?

"Breakfast will be ready in about twenty minutes." He handed me a hot cup of coffee and I took it, avoiding touching his fingers. The rich roast smell wrapped itself around me. This was too domestic, too cozy, too perfect.

Some might call what I felt chemistry, heat, or whatever. But to me, these basic domestic details signaled more to me about core compatibility. Sure his presence was electrifying but observing him cook made my knees weak. His comment last night about wanting a devoted marriage sprang to mind. I guess I wasn't ready to believe he was ready to settle down.

I realized Brandon and I had never had breakfast together in the time we had dated and had stayed over at the other's place. It was becoming clear that Brandon and I had been comfortable with each other but there was something missing from the mix between us. I needed to talk with Brandon and explain. We had left our status up in the air after the disastrous dinner and I hadn't heard from him since then. It was easy to assume it was over, but we needed to have *the talk*.

I caught myself watching Mason as he set plates on the dining table where Roulette lounged underneath. The universe was down right sadistic?

I automatically added an extra place setting at the end of the table. Mason raised an eyebrow in question.

"I um..." This was why it was easier with Brandon, he knew about the extra place setting, as he was nearly part of the family and had known my mother.

"It's in honor of my mother." *Awkward.* "I always have a place for her at my table...Dad started the practice." I took a deep breath. Okay, that was horrible, but done. I glanced at him, a bit sheepish, but he only nodded his head.

"Noted, extra place setting."

I'm not foolish enough to believe a lasting relationship is based on heat. There had to be substance. The words of my mother came to me when I had asked her about boys teasing me. She had gotten serious and told me that some day I would date boys and to remember that she had married the man who was her best friend and who had captured her heart with his love.

Once or twice I thought Brandon was that best friend. But he never was, not really. Brandon was a good and decent guy. But he hadn't captured my heart with his love by any stretch.

I sat at the table and was studying my coffee as if the answers to my life were in the depths of the bitter beverage. Mason was seduction in motion and his comforting me in his arms last night had awakened something in me that reverberated in my dreams, even chased away the nightmares. But, he wasn't where my attention needed to be focused. He was a tempting distraction.

"Not a morning person?" Mason slid into the chair facing me.

"A bit overwhelmed to wake up and find a chef preparing breakfast." I tried for a light tone despite my heavy thoughts.

"Part of my body guard services." He smiled and winked. "It was quiet last night. Hope you got some sleep. Heaven knows you need it after everything you've been through." The mention of sleep brought my dream to mind and I pushed that down before I started blushing. *Hey, it was better than dreams of Pastor Tom's murder, so I guess I couldn't complain.*

"I slept pretty good, considering. Thank you. I don't think I'd have slept at all if I'd been alone." That was all true. *Stay to safe topics, safe ground.* I wanted to ask about the retractable baton he had. He seemed very competent with it as if he had plenty of practice. My neighbor seemed to be more than just a photographer and sometime poker player. But I didn't feel like personal topics were safe right now.

The doorbell rang and I went to answer without wondering who would be stopping by early on a Saturday morning. As if my thoughts had conjured him, I opened the door to Brandon. He looked past me and saw Mason sitting at my table sipping coffee... barefoot.

Wasn't this cozy. At least I was dressed in the least appealing clothes possible, so this couldn't be misconstrued. I noticed Mason's clothes from last night folded on the couch. Too late, Brandon followed my gaze and his face reddened. Wouldn't you know the succulent aroma of the Quiche in the oven began to filter around the living room too.

"I came by to talk, but I guess I'm too late. I didn't believe Loring when he said you had eyes for some neighbor. I thought all the years we've known each other would mean more to you." I had to get control of this situation. I didn't need a scene after my very home had been invaded and I was doing my level best to keep focused and not fall apart.

"Brandon, this is Porsche's boyfriend, and he's my new neighbor. He also stayed in the guest bedroom because I had a break in last night. Please don't make this more than it is." Yeah, I neglected to tell him about the entire embrace and my scintillating dreams. I could only deal with so much at one time.

Mason walked over and shook Brandon's hand. "Mason Sheridan, nice to meet you. It was late last night when the police finally left. Julienne insisted on staying here and her aunt and uncle agreed only if I stayed in the guest room."

He grabbed his folded clothes and shoes. "I'll be heading back over to my place now." I had to hand it to him. He pulled off the friendly helpful non-threatening guy next door when needed. Roulette ran over when Mason picked up her leash and I bent down and got a lick on the cheek and said goodbye to the sweet dog.

Brandon and I watched as Mason paused with the door nearly closed. "Julie, you really need to call and talk to Porsche." The look he leveled me was absent of the friendly guy and was all serious business. *Alrighty then.*

Once the door was closed for a few seconds Brandon ran a hand through his sandy hair. "You expect me to believe a guy like that stayed the night and nothing happened?" I can only imagine what kind of guy he thought Mason was because I probably had some of those thoughts myself, but I didn't want to talk about that.

"Brandon, I'm going to ignore that you just called me a liar and implied I'm a slut. We certainly need to talk – that's what you wanted, right?" He swallowed and watched Mason from my living room window unlocking his door across the street and disappear inside.

He eventually sat at the table where I had sat with Mason a few minutes ago.

"Look, I know I bumbled the other night."

Okay, that was a start.

He licked his lips and leaned his elbows on the table. "I wanted the night to go perfectly, but it was bad timing. A lot of stress and tension."

"Sure, the events of the week could've influenced the mood, I suppose." I wasn't going to sweep his attitude towards my dreams under a rug.

He frowned, his eyebrows scrunching in.

"I don't think we were working out, if we are honest. Think about it, we haven't spent much quality or intimate time together for a while." I paused and he jumped in.

"It's that job..." I held up my hand and cut him off.

"Brandon, we want different things in life. I love you. But, that's become more a love I feel for an old friend, not a lover. I want the best for you...and it's not me." I thought it best to frame it this way. I knew I wouldn't get anywhere explaining why the proposal typified his mentality and thoughtless attitude.

I couldn't keep myself from comparing him to Mason, not physically but temperament, and the most basic tenants of who they were. The differences between Brandon and I seemed clearer in contrast to Mason. I couldn't explain how when I barely knew my neighbor, but even the break-in last night showed a fundamental difference. Brandon didn't even ask me about it after I explained, but Mason empathized with what I'd been through.

"You need somebody who wants to stay put, start a family and do the domestic thing. I want to travel the world and experience other cultures. I want to work in resorts. I want to wait to start a family." I didn't say how I wasn't sure about having kids at all because right now it wasn't even on my radar and might never.

"Are you sure this smooth talker next door isn't what's happened? You know he isn't going to stay around. His type are fast and loose." I surprised myself when I wanted to defend Mason, but to my credit, I didn't go there.

"This is about you and me. Can you look me in the eyes and tell me you think the last six months we have been a close couple?" I was trying to be reasonable and keep things civil.

"We could've been if you didn't insist on a career rather than a job. You don't want what we could be, you've pulled away."

He had stood up and now was at the door. "I hear you loud and clear. You've wanted anything but what I have to offer. So let's just rip the bandage off quickly. I never thought I would be saying this, but it's over between us, you've made sure of that." He slammed the door and I heard him drive away.

The door slamming was the most heat he'd shown in several months between us. He turned the situation around to blame me and that was okay. I'd give him that after finding Mason lounging around my house.

The oven timer dinged, the quiche was done and it smelled tantalizing and decadent. The universe clearly had it out for me today.

I took a slice of the quiche and sat at my table alone to eat it. I took a chunk and raised my fork to the empty place setting to honor my mother before popping it in my mouth. It was delicious. Of course.

In the space of twenty minutes, I had sat at this same table with Mason in his smoky seductive glory sharing a domestic moment and then broke up with my boyfriend. Now I was eating Mason's gourmet quality Quiche with Gruyère cheese and bacon bits. What was worse, once the door slammed I wondered if I was right in breaking up with Brandon. I knew what I was getting into with him. *When had my life gotten so complicated?*

The doorbell rang again. I threw the door open, thinking it was one of the two troublesome men in my life and I was fully ready to let out my frustration when a badge was flashed in my face. It was that detective again.

"Detective Lawrence, ma'am. I need to ask you a few questions." If he expected me to invite him in, he was out of luck. Men.

"It is my day off. What's the problem?" I purposely held the door only partially open.

"Where were you last night?" He took his sunglasses off and stared at me, eyes hard. I swallowed and was suddenly aware of my hands perspiring.

"I...I was at the club house here for most of the evening and then I was with police officers because my home was broken into." I didn't like this at all. What happened that he was here and asking such questions?

He immediately got on his cell phone and from his side of the conversation, he wasn't happy. He hung up and turned his full scrutiny my way again. He took out a small pocket notepad.

"So, names of anyone who saw you last night at the night club." His pencil poised to write.

"Clubhouse, not a night club. We have a clubhouse here for the townhome owners." I gave the names of my neighbors including Mason who rarely had me out of his site, which now I was rather grateful about. I wondered how Delores and Beverly would feel about being interrogated by the detective. It could go either way, they may think it a hoot and check off a life experience, or they could feel insulted. I prayed Delores wouldn't ask to be frisked.

"We found an item of yours at a crime scene." He glared at me as if challenging me to explain.

"That can't be." It flew out of my mouth without thought.

He lifted his cell phone with a photo of an evidence bag. I squinted at the picture of an I.D. badge in a plastic baggie. *My resort badge.* My heart skipped several beats and I wondered if somebody could actually die from bad news. Not in a romantic sense...lover gets word of soul mate's death in war and drops dead on the spot, but the very real possibility I could just perish solely from shock.

How the hell could my badge be anywhere but my purse?

"Whaaaaaat crime scene?" I didn't care if I appeared upset to the detective. I was rattled. My mind started a little mantra, "please not a murder" over and over.

"One of the resort employees was found stabbed with an ice pick." He held my gaze.

No. This just couldn't be happening. Somebody I probably knew, maybe even worked beside. I didn't know every single employee by name, but I interacted with most of them. My mind tried to process how my badge was with an employee and came up blank...as blank as the day my mother passed away.

"Do you mind if I come in and look around?"

"Not without a search warrant and my lawyer present." I must have been on auto-pilot and my survival instincts in full engagement because I hadn't even given it a thought before the words surged out of my mouth.

His left eyebrow tried to touch his receding hairline.

"Whooooo?" My voice went back to nearly a stutter but in soprano.

His eyes narrowed, watching. "Anete in food service...stabbed with an ice pick."

I heard a gasp and realized that was me sucking in air.

"I have witnesses saying you spoke with her the morning after Pastor Drake's murder on the walk around the lake, and again when she was waiting tables. What happened, she realized you killed Drake and she could prove it? Were you trying to figure out how much she saw but just decided to eliminate that threat, be on the safe side?"

Wait, what?! She probably realized who the killer was and it got her killed. Yeah, that was clear to me, since she was first on the scene to discover the murder. Why didn't she tell me, or the police? Oh lord, I hope she didn't try to make a deal and revealed how much she knew. Now she was dead and I was on the hook for her death too.

"I am in management, so I talk with employees regularly, it's part of my job. As management, I also was concerned about her suffering from the trauma. Did your witnesses tell you I got with Human Resources to have a trauma counselor come in for the employees? If you have any further questions you can contact my lawyer." I closed the door on the detective, gently. I checked my purse and found my work badge gone, and only my badge.   My purse was here last night when I was at the clubhouse and walking with Mason...and during the break in.

Chapter Seventeen

The detective's visit was enough to send the average girl into a comfort food binge with the curtains drawn to shut out the cruel world.

On top of the break-in, seeing Pastor Tom's dead body that still haunted me, the bomb threat at the hotel, and then the cherry on top of my life was Mason and Brandon. I wanted to shut the world off and crawl back in bed and pull the covers up. Yeah, that sounded good.

Before I knew it, I was crying. I soaked a few tissues before deciding I couldn't wallow in tears all day. My eyes were scratchy and felt hot. I had to get my mind off everything, particularly the inner voice ringing in my head that I might have made a terrible mistake letting Brandon go without more of a fight.

There wasn't enough sheet music nor movies to get my mind distracted. *Arrrgggg.* I would have to resort to drastic measures. I grabbed a bag from my closet and carefully locked up my home to face my fate for the next hour.

The workout room in the upstairs of the clubhouse hadn't changed since I had last visited...a few months ago. I've been busy and not had the time. I drew up short when I spotted Delores on the treadmill doing a fast walk. I remembered Delores had gone to dinner last night with the Pastor Drake's secretary.

She turned off the treadmill and joined me at the stationary bicycle. I restrained myself with great effort from immediately asking for all the details of her dinner. She didn't look happy if that scowl was any indication.

"I heard your house was broken into last night, honey. I'm so sorry. Was anything taken?" I really didn't want to think about the break in and that note sitting on my bed. A chill ran down my spine.

"No, I haven't found anything missing so far." I didn't want to go into how my missing badge was now evidence in a second murder...or the ominous note on my bed.

"Well thank goodness for that. Maybe you scared them away when you got home." She paused and silence began to stretch out. I stared out the window without actually seeing the trees dressed in their autumn glory. Delores broke the tense silence. "I wanted to tell you about my dinner last night. I was going to call you but...well."

"I really appreciate your getting in touch with Meredith. I hope it was good to reconnect aside from

Pastor Tom." That's me feeling guilty for having used my friends to save myself.

"In fact, it was really good to see her again. We've set up a monthly date to get together. I forgot how much we have in common." I think I actually let out a sigh of relief.

"Meredith was surprisingly talkative about Pastor Drake. She was about to resign, she didn't want to work for him anymore. He had secrets and Meredith isn't stupid nor blind."

Delores paused a few moments and fiddled with her t-shirt before continuing. "His wife was definitely leaving him and the elders were trying to talk her out of it for the sake of the ministry and the church. So that question is answered." She spoke with a snap. I glanced at her and noted her eyebrows scrunched. I returned my gaze to the window, successfully avoiding eye contact. I don't know if it made Delores more comfortable telling me, but it made me feel better.

"As for a monthly meeting with some...um...wife swappers, she overheard the elders confronting Pastor Drake about something that could have been such a thing. Meredith says Pastor was rather indignant about their questioning and defended himself with references to David having multiple wives and Solomon had hundreds of concubines." She took a shaky breath and I glimpsed her fists clenching.

"As for the girl Cynthia...Meredith says she remembers a teen who would have counseling sessions once a week with Pastor. She was withdrawn and shy but started to blossom in the course of the counseling. Cynthia started dressing better, rather than just ratty jeans and sloppy shirts. She began to wear nice slacks and tops or a few dresses, got her hair styled and began to wear a little makeup. Meredith thought she was interacting more with her peers and just coming out of her shell. But, she noticed how Drake would compliment her in more personal ways. Meredith swears the looks between them became secretive." She paused. I didn't say a word for fear she would stop sharing, eyes focused directly out the window. I couldn't imagine how hard that was for her to repeat.

She began pacing. "Then the counseling sessions just stopped one day and Meredith thought perhaps Pastor realized the girl had developed a crush on him and ended the sessions." She cleared her throat but continued her tight pacing of a few steps each way.

"One day a few months back, Pastor got a call on his cell phone while Meredith was in his office and she believes it was the girl's voice on the phone. But, Drake claimed it was his wife. Anyway, Meredith found out later that the girl had committed suicide when Pastor Drake tasked her to send flowers to the family." Delores was quiet and stopped pacing. I felt like she had just handed off this mess and wanted nothing more to do with it.

"Thank you, I know that was hard for you." I didn't know what else to say.

"Meredith kept the address of Cynthia's parents where she sent the flowers, here?" Delores's voice was tight as she handed me a sticky note with an address.

I hesitated but rushed to get a question out. "She was looking for another job you said. How did she feel about his murder? She give you any hint, like an initial thought that a particular person killed him maybe?" It was a long shot, but perhaps Meredith unloaded a burden to her old friend.

Delores was quiet for so long I thought maybe I shouldn't have pushed with that question. *Uh oh, had I gone too far?*

"She didn't say anything like that. But..." I bit my tongue to keep from jumping in to drag it out of her. I didn't want to make a neighbor mad, or madder at me. "I don't think she was particularly distressed by his death. She wasn't like the Meredith I remember."

"She needs you I suspect." I smiled at her and we looked each other in the eyes.

"Well, I have to go now." She quickly turned and left.

I took my time with a light jog on the treadmill and thought about what Delores had just shared.

I had to concede, if I suspected Crandel as the Youth Director having a reason to permanently stop Drake from taking advantage of the church girls, then Meredith had just as much of a reason, maybe more. She knew about the rocky marriage and at least suspected his swinging activities too. But, as far as I knew she hadn't been at the networking event. Still, I wondered about Delores' comment that the woman was changed, different.   On the other hand, looking for another job to leave was healthy. I would add her to my list as a last resort only, for Delores' sake.

Walking back after my short workout, I considered Mason's parting admonition to call Porsche. What was that about? And the look he had given me? Now that I thought back on it, it seemed like he was angry. Yes, his eyes had a glint of anger in them before he closed the door. I felt a moment of panic. This was all too much. Maybe it would be good to call Porsche and unload.

My house was locked up as I had left it, which was a small consolation. I immediately went upstairs and got out my greeting card file. I have a greeting card for every occasion and store them in an accordion file folder by topic. I scour every store's card section and buy the best. I love having a wide selection at my fingertips. I chose a Thank You card with an adorable mouse on it and quickly wrote a few words to Delores, addressed and stamped it. I slipped the address Delores had given me into a new file on Pastor Tom.

I was restless, even after a short jog. I showered and ran to the store for groceries and mail the card in a mail drop at the store.

While dashing through the store, my dad called on my cell phone. Several fellow-shoppers gave me strong looks as I fought to keep him from visiting. It would be nice to see him again, but I simply couldn't handle one more pressure point, even from my family. My dad would mean well, but he would nag me to leave my job. Not what I needed right now. I hung up with a promise to keep him informed.

I returned home about forty-five minutes later to find Felicia on my doorstep with an overnight case, guess she didn't have a key like Aunt Regina. I parked my car in the garage and grabbed my shopping bag of groceries. Felicia strolled into the garage with a serious look on her face. Today she had opted for red jeans that showed off her plush curves with a cashmere scoop neck sweater in tan and chandelier earrings.

"Hear you had a break-in last night, I'm here to keep you safe." I barked out a laugh that my girly-girl cousin, who felt chipping one of her meticulous nails was a dire emergency, would provide any protection.

"Mason called mom. They have really hit it off, you know. They decided that we could have a nice little slumber party since there is strength in numbers. Mason will join us for the evening. He's bringing dinner. Oh, and I'm to tell you to call Porsche." Again with the call Porsche bit. *Okay, I got it.*

"It'll be like when we were kids."

"Except I plan to get some sleep and no pillow fights," I warned.

"Well, we'll see about that." She bounced up the stairs to the guest bedroom where I tasked her to change the sheets. Mason was bringing dinner. Guess he wasn't too disturbed about Brandon this morning if he was going to cook again. I resigned myself to his culinary talents yet again. The sacrifices I make.

I finally made that phone call to Porsche in the privacy of my room with the door closed while Felicia was busy on her cell phone with a friend.

"Hi girlfriend, I was hoping you would call." She was cheery. Good so far.

"Porsche, you never told me how your date went with Mason. Don't hold back now, tell me the details." I didn't actually mean that last part. I was taking this one step at a time. Nothing to take your mind off your own failed relationship than to listen about another couple...oh, joy.

"Dear there's nothing to tell. I was all ready to have some fun with him, a fling for a few months. We went to that new Greek restaurant and he was attentive, polite, funny, and a great date. We laughed and the time flew by, except for one thing." This I hadn't expected. I should've known Porsche would have reading men down to a science.

"Really, a problem so soon?"

"He's a perfectly nice guy from what I could tell but he was only interested in you. What you were like growing up, what your dad is like, Brandon and you. If he'd been even remotely interested in me I wanted to put his hard body through a workout, but he wanted to know all about you. If I need some arm candy I may still call him up, but there's no future between us." Of all the scenarios that ran through my head, I didn't remotely consider that. He sure found out about Brandon and I this morning.

"I thought when you didn't say anything about the date that maybe you guys were seeing each other, maybe even serious." She guffawed on the other end.

"I haven't found a guy I want around longer than a few months at best. Remember that doctor lasted a month and a half."

I figured they were perfect for each other. Maybe I wanted to use Porsche as an excuse. I certainly hadn't asked her about her date with him sooner. No wonder I had clung to Brandon even though it was going nowhere. Brandon was safe and predictable. Mason was anything but, and it scared the bejeezus out of me. I swallowed.

"Have you found anything more out from the students or other professors?" I was moving to safe ground.

"I emailed it to you from work so I wouldn't get any of the details mixed up. Check your email. Sooo, are you going to give into temptation with Mason?"

"I don't know. He isn't my type. He's a player and that isn't what I want. You can deal with players without getting burned or heartbroken." I didn't share how my type was shifting a little.

"Do you remember in high school when I had that mystery guy I was dating?" I wasn't sure where this was going, but I remembered. At the time, I thought she was seeing a senior. "Well he was a college guy, five years older than me and I got my heart broke real good. I'm not immune honey. Between us, I think that is why I just date a guy for a while and then kick them out before I get too involved."

"You never told me that. I'm sorry Porsche. Sometimes things just suck." I wasn't sure what else to say, but we could both agree on that.

"I got my house broke into last night and Mason stayed in the spare bedroom." This was my big confession I guess.

"And you thought we were dating and you were tempted even though he isn't your type." I didn't say anything. "Well, we aren't together so don't let it bother you any longer, okay? Thanks for being the friend I can trust with a boyfriend."

"Thanks Porsche for everything. I'll check that email." I hung up and immediately went and printed out her email and put it in the new file along with the address of Seattle Cynthia. I didn't even read Porsche's email because I was really considering adding the few things that were stolen and turning it over the police with my lawyer.

Chapter Eighteen

I washed off the dining table and put a basic tablecloth on it, nothing fancy. Then, I put out what I considered my everyday placemats that weren't the same as the tablecloth but matched okay. I had bought some dog food, a special food and water bowl, and treat bones for Roulette that I stashed away. Roulette was impressive last night and I wanted to reward her.

Felicia had been busy on her phone with several friends. Apparently, she had been scheduled to go out for a girl's night. She was engrossed in discussing the latest gossip so she wouldn't feel left out.

I'd changed earlier in the day from the sweats into jeans and a lightweight white pointelle sweater but now I considered whether I should get those sweats back on before Mason arrived. It didn't happen.

Mason arrived with his arms full of restaurant bags filled with food and a bag from an electronics and hardware store. Roulette trotted in after him, her eyes following the food.

I made myself busy with the food and setting everything out on the table. Mason cornered me in the kitchen, his eyes stern and his mouth set. He was still wearing that button down shirt and jeans and I had to admit he looked good. I pictured him in an Armani suit for a second. *Oh my. Danger in that direction.*

"Please tell me you called Porsche?" His hands on his hips. He was like a pit bull that wasn't letting go of something.

"Yes, we had a good talk." I was studying the kitchen floor and contemplating whether I should mop it tonight.

"I'm glad to hear that." He nudged my chin up so I was looking into his eyes. "We can talk more about that later. Let's eat ma bichette, hope you like Italian." I swallowed hard. He already had a nickname for me and it made my heart skip a beat, *my little doe.* When my aunt invited him to dinner he must have realized our French heritage. Or, knowing Aunt Regina, she told him all about my family.

"Looks like Felicia's taking the guest room. You don't need to stay tonight."

"I'll stay on the couch." He raised a hand and stopped me before I could object. "No arguments. Unless of course Brandon is going to be staying to look after you ladies?" There it was, the tangible difference between them. Brandon never acknowledged the break-in, let alone I might be scared or even in danger.

"Dinner will be on the table in just a few minutes." I didn't want to talk about Brandon, and especially not with him. I could feel his gaze follow me as I turned toward the kitchen, but he let the topic drop. I took a dog treat to Roulette and she rolled over for it. She was a special dog.

We had a great meal full of chatting between the three of us with a very nice Sangiovese wine Mason had also picked up. Felicia was fascinated with his gambling and I began to worry she was considering taking up Texas Hold'em and lose all her money. She worked part time in a clothing boutique downtown and she didn't make much and spent most of that in the store on clothes she couldn't resist.

"I read online you dated Moisha. What was she like?" I shouldn't have been surprised that Felicia did exactly what I'd done and looked him up online. I wasn't sure I really wanted to hear about his past dating skinny models. Yeah, I keep telling myself I'm not interested, but I don't want his dating rubbed in my face either.

"I accompanied her to a few functions, there's a difference between that and what I consider a date. Moisha's a kind person who's under a lot of pressure from everybody around her."

He looked at me and seemed to come to some decision. "I've gone out with a model here and there, but it was more work than pleasure. I got more name recognition which helped my career as a photographer and they got a bodyguard that the press would never suspect." I found myself staring into his eyes. A bodyguard? He just said he had been more of a bodyguard on the sly for all those models. Could that really be? Then I remembered that retractable baton last night and how he handled it.

"Why would you be a bodyguard? I mean, don't most of them have training like former cops or something?" Felicia plowed ahead without even a passing nod to the idea of treading lightly. He looked a bit uncomfortable and slipped a piece of meatball to Roulette who stayed by his side dutifully.

"Felicia, maybe he doesn't want to talk about it. It isn't any of our business really."

"Somebody broke in here last night and I want to know there's more than testosterone to protect you." She looked at him, "no offense." *I bet.*

"None taken. Felicia makes a good point."

He took a few moments, rubbed his chin. "I was Marine Special Forces. I'm sniper class in firearms, black belt fourth degree in Marine Corps Martial Arts and also Black Belt fifth degree TaeKwonDo. I think I qualify as a bodyguard, how about you?" *Yes, that qualified in my book. Damn, maybe he is a bit like Jason Bourne. A Bourne-Bond hybrid maybe.* I smiled to myself. He raised an eyebrow and I realized the smile showed, and my face grew hot.

Felicia just nodded her head as though she were weighing a job applicant. I wondered if she was trying to compare Brandon and Mason because it was unfair to even attempt it. Brandon was a hometown boy who would've loved a small town life, Mason had been in the military, traveled, experienced life, and lived a far different reality. They were about as opposite as two men could be.

"That'll do." She finally said with a barely veiled appraising look up and down. She wasn't going easy on him. I think she liked having somebody besides her brother Loring to pester. Mason raised an eyebrow and glanced at me as if to say "so glad I pass muster."

I was still getting used to the idea of Mason's military background. Even though I was raised in Colorado Springs with Army and Air Force bases, the Air Force Academy, and the famous NORAD that brought a few Canadian military into town, I'd never had the Air Force cadet dating fever nor was I into the Academy's football team. It wasn't that I didn't support the military; I just wasn't so much for having the regimented mindset in my life. Looking at his shoulder-length hair, I found it hard to imagine him with a buzz cut and a uniform. But that Armani suit sure looked good on him in my imagination.

When we finished dinner he got up and brought the electronics store bag back to the dinner table. "These are audio monitors, one for each of you. I'll be here on the couch and listening through the night." They were baby monitors essentially.

"If either of you call out I'll be up those stairs in a heartbeat. You can turn it on when you're ready to go to sleep so you don't have to worry about my listening to any girl talk you don't want me to hear." He winked at us. I know I blushed, again.

The hardware bag contained deadbolts that looked industrial grade. Mason began installing those on the front and backdoors since the existing locks were clearly not up to par after last night's easy break-in.

Felicia pulled me aside. "Hope you aren't noisy when you dream. It'd be a shame if he ran up the stairs to find you having steamy dreams of him." She smiled a wicked smile.

"I could say the same to you. You looked him up on the internet and gave him the full body scan too. Geez, girl."

"Your dad isn't here to ask about his intentions, so I'm winging it. I'm just looking after you dear." That had me speechless and I walked away shaking my head.

Roulette was given a short walk before we reconvened in more comfort in the living room. Felicia and I took the couch while Mason sat in a chair across from us. The easy going mood from dinner was now focused.

Mason leaned forward in his chair facing me. "You need to fill me in on everything you've found out on Pastor Drake. After the break-in and nasty note last night, you now have a partner on this little investigation of yours."

Chapter Nineteen

I brought down my file and laptop to the couch. Felicia was giddy being included on the information gathered so far.

I told him about Delores's conversation with Meredith and it seems Cynthia was used by the pastor, the wife was on the verge of leaving him. I also related the embrace I had interrupted at the Drake reception, even though I couldn't identify the man. I'd already shared about Robert Crandel and David Babcock at the family dinner, so I summarized them.

By the time I was done, Felicia's eyes were unfocused and she hadn't spoken for quite awhile. I hadn't realized how much I had compiled already. Then again, she had eaten a lot and had sunk into the deep couch cushions, I wasn't sure she was fully awake.

"You've dug up some good gossip with lots of potential. But, in order to give the police more than a handful of conjecture and hearsay, we've got work to do. Of course, you could simply give them what you have so far. It'd still give them something to investigate." He waited for me to answer.

"After you left this morning I was visited by that Detective." I found it hard to tell the rest. "Anete, the gal who found Drake.... Well, she was killed last night, and my resort badge was there in the room...the crime scene. So I don't think they are looking for anybody else to investigate."

"Was that badge here during the break-in?" Mason was quick to ask.

"Yep. Looks like framing me was the reason for the break-in and the warning was a special bonus. Multitasking." I sank back into the couch, attempting to relax.

"How well did you know the girl?" Felicia's look of sympathy made a lump form in my throat.

"I knew her as an employee, but not well otherwise. She's worked for us about two years now. She's from Latvia like many of our staff that we sponsor and provide work visas. She was pretty traumatized by finding him." I know it had gotten to her.

"It gets worse." I hesitated a moment and sat forward. "I spoke to her the morning after the murder and at lunch the other day, and there was a 'witness' who saw it." I did air quotes. "The police think she knew I killed him so I silenced her."

"But, you were at the clubhouse and with me the whole evening." Mason's eyebrows were scrunched and his voice was commanding. Now I could imagine him in the military.

"I told the good detective that, and he took names to verify the times. I don't think he was happy I had an alibi. I don't like being a suspect, the questioning of the staff and interrogating my family. I don't think he'll let the easy solution, me, off-the-hook because of what I've gathered so far. I need more before I turn it over. I could lose my job even if they never arrest me since the members are complaining." I was trying to sound matter-of-fact rather than whiny. Not sure it worked.

"So, the detective thinks the same person killed this Anete too? It would seem too much of coincidence for two different killers I imagine." Both Mason and I stared at Felicia.

"What? Was that wrong?"

"No, you're right. It does seem too much of a coincidence for two unrelated murders at the resort." I smiled at her.

"Which leaves us working with what we have access to and knowledge of...Drake's murder. You have motives for his murder popping up like a mole in that kid's game. But let's look at access and opportunity. There were only a few short minutes that somebody could have killed him, the killer had to be close."

Earlier while Felicia was on the phone I had printed off a file from work I forwarded to my personal email. I grabbed the printout of attendees for the event now and began circling names with a red pen.

"Well, the wife was present along with Crandel and Babcock.   The secretary, Meredith, wasn't there according to this list.   I don't know names of any possible swingers involved, nor any of the girls he may have compromised."   Mason scanned the list and then sighed.

"We definitely need more information.   If one of these three can't be accounted for during your breakout sessions then we 'd have somebody to tell the police about."

"I'm getting a list of the wait staff who were working the buffet lunch.   There are fewer than if it'd been a plated dinner.   Claudia, our Human Resources gal, will get me that.   The staff could tell us where attendees were. I hope."

"We need the staff listing because of their access too. One of them could have had a run-in with him like you and killed him."

"I wish we knew more about the other situations. Those sound volatile enough to lead to his death."

"Do you mean the swingers that we discussed on our walk?"   Mason asked.

"Wow, wait one darned minute.   What are you talking about?   Swingers?   What swingers?"   Felicia chirped.

Mason choked down a laugh.

Felicia had been watching us both.   "So I'm gathering this group isn't swing dancing?"

With a broad grin, Mason explained the concept of swingers.

"Pastor Drake did this? Seriously!" Felicia's eyes were huge.

"We don't know that absolutely yet, but it's a possibility." Mason countered with mirth in his eyes.

I quickly explained to her Nathan's friend, Ramone's customers, and Meredith all providing information that made it highly likely the pastor was indeed involved. I went ahead and included how I had contacted the reporter about the article on local swingers groups.

I fired up my laptop. Mason moved to behind the couch and watched over my shoulder as I checked the email address I had set up solely for contacting the reporter about a contact for the Swingers article he wrote. I had a reply from earlier in the day. I kicked myself for not checking sooner. One of his contacts from his article was willing to talk with me and assist my "research" he gave a phone number to contact him for a phone interview.

I swallowed, unsure what to do with the information now that I had it.

"Were you going to interview the guy or what?" Mason had sat back down and his brow was furrowed.

"I hadn't really thought it through. I don't know how much this guy could really tell me." My voice had gotten soft as doubt filled me.

"We could always just ask to attend as a trial run without making a commitment, like we weren't sure about the idea." I turned to look him in the eyes. He was serious.

"I couldn't....you know...with somebody's spouse...like it was trying on new shoes or something." I was stuttering. His eyebrows had risen as I struggled.

"I'm sure we can both turn the situation to talking and getting information rather than consummating anything." He shrugged his shoulder as if it were no big deal.

My eyes narrowed. Sure.

"How 'bout we contact this person and see how much information we can extract?" He offered.

I shuffled through my notes to shift my focus and drop the subject of the swingers for now.

"Oh, I forgot Porsche had sent me something she found in asking students at her college." I held up my finger to indicate wait a minute. I know many people would have a file on the computer, but I liked having paper.

"Got it." I scanned it first. "Seems a few students went to Drake's church. Only one she found had anything that might help us. This Cynthia gal I heard about had a brother that the family claimed had 'anger management' issues and the rest of the family was known to be in and out of trouble." I kept scanning the email. "Cynthia left to get away from the family drama and had been a big follower of Pastor Tom's radio program so she came here to join his church." I scrunched my forehead in thought.

"Quit scowling girl, it will cause wrinkles." Felicia was quick to comment.

I looked at Felicia and then Mason back and forth. "We could really use somebody, *a girl*, to attend the church and go to the Sunday school, talk with the teen youth group members that Cynthia knew. Somebody will figure out who I am since I was in the paper, or I would do it." I raised my eyebrows in question.

Felicia's eyes grew big. "Me? You want me to attend his church? I'm no good at the sneaky stuff and I can't lie. Remember Carl Packard's mailbox?" In Felicia's defense, she'd been studying all night for finals and the mailbox wasn't badly damaged...much. But we found out just how terrible she was at lying under pressure that day.

"It isn't sneaky, anybody can attend a church. They're open to the public and you don't need an invitation. You're only checking out the church, which is true so you don't have to lie. They probably have something happening during the week so you can jump in right away." Mason was looking uncomfortable with Felicia's involvement so I forged ahead quickly. "Just try and get into the same college or youth group Cynthia was and listen. Maybe ask a few questions that anybody would be curious about. You know how to gossip girl, that's all you're going to do."

Felicia began to smile, then a giggle bubbled up. "It's true, anybody can attend the church and gossiping is more common than a cold. I can do this."

We made our plans. Felicia would call the church in the morning and see if there was a mid-week worship or prayer group that she could jump into. Mason would come by the resort and get a membership to mingle and gossip with staff mostly. We could start with the wait staff I remembered from that day until we got the complete list from Claudia. We could call Cynthia's family if we managed to find phone number now that we had her full name and an address in Seattle. I purposely didn't mention the swingers group again and hoped it would be forgotten. I also planned on staying quiet about Brandon's visit this morning.

Felicia took off up the stairs to her guest room to drop off her baby monitor and a few of her things and I was left alone with Mason. His words from earlier in the kitchen that we would talk more later came back to me. I was pretty sure I couldn't outrun him, chicken that I am.

I went into the kitchen to begin the popcorn and get the snacks all prepared for the movie. Finally, a break from the seriousness. Mason stood next to the island and watched me ignore him. I avoided making any eye contact, but I was aware of exactly where he was. He finally moved closer and I tensed. He leaned close and in a low rumble he spoke, his lips brushing my ear.

"Once things settle down and you're recovered from breaking up, I'd like to take you out for dinner." He put his forefinger to my lips when I began to say something. I couldn't breathe. "Just a date. Dinner and dancing, maybe."

I cleared my throat, not trusting my voice to be steady. "Yeah, uh hmm." *Eloquent, that's me!*

Chapter Twenty

Mason walked me to work in the morning after Roulette was secured back at his house. I got to see him in a dark steel-blue Armani suit in reality. The sight was better than in my dreams. I tried to convince myself that Armani made all men look good, but I wasn't buying it. I was feeling guilty over my dreams then drooling over him in the suit as if I was cheating on Brandon.

I got Mason a membership and showed him around the grounds, which drew attention from most women in the vicinity...and a few men. Yeah, he really looked damn good in the suit. I had a growing suspicion he would be able to find out more information from the staff than I ever could on Pastor Tom and the whereabouts of attendees at the time of the murder.

I set Mason loose on the Resort and their staff and I now found myself staring into space at my desk remembering last night, the last whiffs of spicy cologne lingering to tantalize me.

We eventually watched a movie, all three of us. I don't remember what we watched, I couldn't breathe with Mason sitting next to me on the couch, close enough for his spicy cologne to envelope me, distract me.

Our hands would brush when grabbing popcorn from the bowl and I thought the air around us was so electric it would ignite. I finally coaxed Roulette to settle on the couch between us with another doggie treat. She was very smart and eager to get that milk bone.

I shook my head, I needed to think about something else. I wondered how Felicia was managing. She was starting her mission to infiltrate the church and gather more proof of the reported impropriety with Cynthia or the other young girls. Plus getting more information on the four suspects associated with the church, wife Sarah, the radio partner, church's youth director, and his secretary Meredith. But it would be after work before I would find out how she managed.

Which left the swingers contact for me to followup with...in the privacy of my office I hoped. I locked my office door and sat staring at my cell phone with the number keyed in. I just needed to hit dial. I didn't dare use the resort phone, that would be a disaster if there was caller ID on the other end. I finally took a shaky breath and dialed.

"Hello, I was given this number by Arlene at the paper. She said you would be expecting my call." I crossed my fingers.

"Yes, dear. She got my permission for you to call me directly. How can I help you with your book?" The cultured male voice conjured an image of a Shakespearean actor.

"I'm looking at the interpersonal dynamics of swinging rather than academic facts." I really hadn't thought how I was going to approach this, and now I was scrambling. "It's really for a fiction book...my couple in the story is looking at a swinger's group. Can you tell me how issues like jealousy are alleviated?"

"Fiction...okaaay. Most have been married for many years already and need to be trusting, secure, and honest with each other. If you feel jealous, this isn't for you." His tone was sincere. Even if Pastor Tom's wife didn't like the lifestyle, it sounded like jealousy from other women in the group wasn't likely if this man was to be believed. But, it still left the wife possibly jealous or getting even.

"Right, but the husband...in my story...is more eager for this lifestyle than the wife."

"We don't encourage participation unless both are agreeable. You should discuss with your husband all aspects first. You can opt to not do any swapping and keep each other as partners until you're both comfortable and want to take that step. This is meant to accentuate your marital relationship not be a Band-

Aid for problems that exist." *Wait, what?* I ran a hand over my face.

"Hold up, this is for a book, a story. Not about me, I'm not even married."

"Sure, I get it."

"Do you have many devout religious people and how do they reconcile this lifestyle? Because the couple in my story are sincere in their faith." My hands were sweating. Was I obvious I was asking about Pastor Tom?

"There are people of faith who have found peace with the additional adult entertainment and expression. I think you'll find we have very respectable members." This wasn't going the way I had hoped. How could I possibly get any information about Pastor Tom this way? He seemed to think I was shopping for a group to join. I needed a different angle.

"See, here's the thing. My fictional couple is really devout churchgoers, and...the experience isn't good. I figure one of them, say the husband, gets blackmailed because of his faith or maybe the wife isn't reconciled with her beliefs and gets attached to another member. Something like that, *for the sake of my story,* how realistic is that? Have you run into such cases?"

"Blackmail or marriage issues because of swinging are rare in my experience. I don't think you have anything to worry about. We use nicknames rather than our everyday names and we agree to a privacy policy. If a marriage breaks down, they had problems before joining our group." I doubted a code name would keep anybody from realizing who Pastor Tom was since he'd been on the cover of *Time* magazine last year. I wasn't getting anywhere over the phone.

"I could arrange for you and your husband to attend one night, I would need you to agree to our privacy policy. We have a night later this week. Talk it over and call me if you're interested." We hung up and I was more frustrated than ever. I kicked my desk and swore. The nerve of that man to think I was shopping. I was trying to get information without actually attending a swinger meeting.

I drummed my fingers on the desk. How can I follow this lead without having to be part of it? If I knew where this gathering was going to take place later in the week and just observe who arrived, I could compare to who attended the event where Pastor Tom was stabbed. But I had no idea how to accomplish that without actually showing up with a guy. The thought alone terrified me.

If only I knew where it would be without calling the man back.

Chapter Twenty-one

I spent the afternoon training with Hotel Guest Services. Mason had spent the day around the resort and I spotted him once at a patio café chatting up the employees. I marveled at how easily he made friends.

Mason walked me home again. I was beginning to feel like a child walked to and from school. But, if I had to be escorted I couldn't have asked for better.

I was handed off to Felicia who accompanied me to the mailboxes. I hoped to see my neighbors and catch up on any new information. I was afraid they might not talk with Felicia along. *Touchy, like street informants.* I chuckled at the thought of my "mature" neighbors acting like police snitches.

I took a long time checking my mail but eventually, Nathan strolled over. We exchanged pleasantries before getting to business. He seemed to accept Felicia without question, he likely already knew she was family.

"Talk to your friend?" There was no easy way to slide into the conversation.

"Yeah. We were right." He looked around and made a show of taking out his mailbox key, not facing me.

"Swingers. No definite proof of Drake involvement, just heavily hinted at." His mail in hand, he turned.

"No proof doesn't help. He have any other participant names?" I looked around too, glancing at shadows.

"He didn't want to tell me, but it was Peter Patterson who invited him. Corporate Legal Eagle type." He coughed and spoke the next too loud. "Yeah, see you at the next game night."

"Now that was strange. Is he always like that?" Felicia commented as she watched him dart away.

"Nope. Maybe he's enjoying passing messages and feeling a bit covert." That was all I could think of.

That side trip completed, we convened at my place. I made my easy Beef Stroganoff with ground chuck, a splash of nice left-over wine, mushroom soup, and sour cream. I tossed a kale salad with pecans and cranberries from a bag-of-salad kit and paired it all with a Bordeaux and Chardonnay wines.

I'm an efficient cook, not elaborate, and had everything done from beginning to end in thirty minutes or so. I was consciously paying Mason back for the quiche he made the other day. Besides, he and Felicia were helping me out by staying with me. Not only would I have been scared, but I would have been sad, lonely, and maybe even depressed after Brandon's angry words. I found myself almost calling him twice at work today, but stopped myself. I could see how I'd been leaning on him, and that wasn't fair to him.

Felicia and Mason had set the table and I was surprised to see a gold tablecloth and napkins had been dug out and dressed up the table.

"This is fancy, we celebrating or something?" I asked.

"I thought we could do something a little different tonight." Felicia had taken the serving bowl with the Stroganoff and sat it down then faced me. "How about a relaxing nice dinner...and a music night? We haven't done that for ages."

"What's a music night?" Mason stopped pouring wine, waiting for an answer.

I opened my mouth to speak, but not fast enough. "Sometimes at family gatherings, we would each do something musical." Felicia supplied.

Mason quirked one eyebrow up. "What musical talents do you two claim?"

"Felicia sings and plays piano. She has a lovely voice." Although she hadn't sung in public since winning a talent contest her High School senior year.

"Julienne plays Clarinet, has since she was six or something. She's quite good. Mom got her to play in the symphony for three nights when an outbreak of the flu swept through the wind section. Julienne could have continued playing for them, but she turned it down." Felicia looked me in the eyes and her eyebrows danced up and down a few times. I groaned inwardly. I didn't need her talking me up to Mason.

Mason smiled bright. "I knew your aunt Regina plays viola in the symphony, but you too? I'm impressed."

"We're a musical family. Uncle Lars plays accordion, cousin Loring plays the saxophone, my dad even manages the trumpet." I said.

"Remember how Loring thought he was going to be the next Kenny G? He thought it would get him dates in high school, but he hated practicing." Felicia chuckled.

We sat at one end of the table, taking the same places as last night and I passed the salad.

"I play guitar. Took lessons all through high school. I thought if I played in a band I could get dates. At that age, the band groupie thing sounded awesome. Found out I liked playing and didn't care for groupies." He passed the Stroganoff.

He didn't like the groupies? Here I was about to conclude this tale was the origin of his playboy status. A vision appeared in my head, completely unwanted, of Mason in jeans playing a guitar with his hair cascading around his face and a soulful look in his eyes. I mentally slapped myself.

He likes dressing in fine suits, competes in professional poker tournaments, provides bodyguard services to models, happens to be a photographer, and also enjoys playing a guitar. I couldn't reconcile the various personas to the man wearing black denim and a royal blue button down shirt who was prior military. The more I knew, the more of a mystery he presented.

"Felicia, why the interest in a music night? I didn't think you enjoyed them much." I focused my gaze on her.

"Well, you know my assignment was to gain access to the church, see if there were any activities I could join this week." She cleared her throat. "They were having choir rehearsals today and I need to practice three songs for this Sunday."

Mason and I stared at her. I think my mouth was gaping open.

"What? I infiltrated successfully and phase one is checked off."

"You realize that, with any luck, we'll have our investigation done and ready to turn over to the police before Sunday, right?" I didn't want her to get in too deep. Besides, Aunt Regina would blame me when she didn't go to mass because she was helping me provide murder suspects.

"Sure, but I have a solo part and I want to do it. I forgot how much I liked singing."

"Did you find out any information about our suspects?" Mason cut to the chase.

"Oh, *that* was easy. The older women have a few suspicions, but the gals around my age have known a girl here or there who claimed to be cozy with the pastor but would end up leaving the church. There was one gal, in particular, they each knew who insisted she would marry Pastor Tom."

Felicia's explanation was punctuated with occasional murmurs of "mmmmm" and Mason had let out a "yum". I was pleased to see them enjoying my cooking. Between bites of salad, I kept her talking. "Did you get a name for this determined girl?"

"Was it Cynthia?" Mason added.

"Yep, that's the gal. They all figured she was living in a fantasy." Felicia said.

"They didn't consider maybe she was being strung along or lied to?" I couldn't help the indignant tone.

"They said she was rather gullible and even zealous. They seemed to accept how the pastor got close to some, maybe too casual, but not as *intimate* as we're suspecting."

I shook my head in wonder.

"Anything on the wife or others?"

"Well, the older ladies had plenty of gossip on them. Wife was definitely leaving him and sides were being drawn over keeping the pastor if he was divorced or kicking him out on his ear. They all knew Babcock and Drake could barely be in a room together without an argument, but they couldn't agree on whose fault it was. Seems Babcock drank, maybe too much, and some felt that was justification to muscle him out of the radio program even if he'd made it successful." She stopped to take a few bites and a sip of wine before continuing.

"So the Youth Director guy, Crandel.   One of the girls swears he's gay and she saw him in downtown Denver holding hands with a guy. I say maybe it was him, or maybe not. But, most felt he tried to avoid Pastor Tom at every chance."

"Do you think he's gay?" Mason asked her.

"Could be. Solid maybe on that." She shoveled a forkful of salad into her mouth. I thought about him during the funeral reception and couldn't really say one way or the other. Mason looked at me and I shrugged my shoulders in answer.

"He was avoiding Pastor Tom, huh?" I mused. How had this church survived, let alone grown to over ten thousand members with such fighting and drama?

"What about the secretary?" Mason tossed out.

"Oh, that's interesting. Everyone was shocked when word got out she was looking for another job. They all swear had a case of hero worship. Sounds like they thought she was a sad spinster with a crush." She stopped eating and used her fork for emphasis. "It really sounded more like she was so blindly *devoted* to Pastor Drake. But, something broke the spell and she couldn't even *work for him* anymore." She nodded her head at the end for emphasis.

"Meredith could've found out about Cynthia or one of the other girls and in an angry fit she comes down to the conference center and kills him." Mason speared some salad with his fork.

"What broke her spell...Drake and the questionable relationship with the girls, or something else, and why now? But the real question is, could she have killed him...that's such a drastic change in her feelings and faith?" Mason asked, but I sure didn't have an answer. I shrugged and shook my head.

"Well, I keep thinking his wife Sarah is a good bet. First, there's Drake leading Cynthia on and maybe others too. Plus the swinger's situation." I took another bite before continuing.

"Babcock could've killed over being squeezed out of the radio syndication. That smacks of betrayal and people have killed for less. If Pastor Tom used Babcock's drinking as the excuse in light of his own escapades with Cynthia and swingers, I can see how it could've driven Babcock over the edge." I took a drink of wine and another bite of the Stroganoff. There was a pause in the discussion, each of us mulling over the various people in this puzzle.

"We can't forget about Crandal. If he's gay, Drake could've held that over his head to keep his mouth shut over his behavior with the girls until Crandal'd had enough and killed him." Felicia finished with a sigh, pushing the last of her salad around.

"Seems we haven't eliminated any of our cast of suspects. We've got plenty of motives for each of them, though." I wasn't sure if that was enough to convince the police to consider somebody other than me for the murder.

We briefly discussed the ability to kill with the ice sculpture and felt his drunken state combined with my knee to his privates rendered him easy for most any man or woman to surprise him with a good shove.

"Which brings us to opportunity," Mason added after his last bite of Stroganoff. He pushed his clean plate away. I felt happy at the sight. I had repaid him for that amazing quiche, even if I got the better meal.

"Sarah was seen down the side corridor outside the restrooms talking with a man a few minutes before the murder." He ticked off the suspects on his fingers. "Babcock was seen hanging at the back of the breakout session room near the door, but couldn't say if he was coming, going, or just trying to stay awake by stretching his legs. Crandel apparently smokes and was puffing away just outside, but that was early enough he could have slipped in and not rejoined his session." Three fingers, three suspects.

"Is there an outside door in the buffet room he might have come and gone via?" He continued.

"Not in the buffet room, but down the hall towards the very back. I might've missed anybody making their way in and out by that entry. Usually, the staff are the only ones that know it exists." Too many options still.

"Which provides an unobserved entry for Crandel from his smoke break, and maybe even Meredith too." Mason conjectured making four fingers. "But we haven't considered the resort staff themselves. Those working at the luncheon had opportunity."

"I have a hard time thinking of somebody I work with being a killer. Did you pick up on anyone today while you staked out the resort?" I had to come to grips with the idea of a staff member potentially being the culprit.

"I didn't get any tingling spidey-sense if that's what you're asking. But one of your servers is a member of Drake's church. Crystal loved gossiping about how the staff was particularly touched by the tragedy. Crystal told everyone that her beloved Pastor Drake would be at the networking leadership luncheon. If somebody on your staff wanted an opportunity, they knew ahead of time he would be there." Mason's brows were drawn together and it was the closest to a scowl I'd seen for him.

"You seem concerned about that." I wanted to know more.

"That could've broadened the list to not only staff,but your staff's friends and family. You said there was a back door that could've been used to enter. Well, anybody who knew Drake would be in attendance could've used that door and waited for you to leave him alone and vulnerable." Mason stared directly at me. That also meant a larger suspect pool of people who could've broken into my home too.

"All I want is to provide a list of some viable alternatives to the police with enough solid potential they can't ignore it."

"We're getting close to being done, I hope. We've now determined opportunity is wide open since it was fairly well known Drake would be there and the back door allowed uncontrolled access. We have several motives discovered. As for the means...that was seized upon with the ice sculpture being handy."

"I think the means should include the capability of killing somebody." It slipped out without a thought.

"That is very true, but hard for us sitting here to really determine. If it is true that anybody has it within them to kill another if pushed hard enough..." He let the thought take flight.

"Where does that leave us?" Felicia asked.

"The swingers and contacting Cynthia's family." Mason provided.

"Well...I called the swinger's contact today and without sounding like a reporter seeking a sensational angle on Pastor Tom to sell papers I didn't get anywhere." I found it difficult to look at either of them.

"Your contact didn't want to talk to you?" Felicia said.

I cleared my throat, shifted in my chair, and hoped I wasn't beat-red. "I talked to a guy who organizes a local group. It became a sales pitch and I couldn't get him to just give me specific information." I wasn't happy when Felicia started giggling like when we did slumber parties. I shot a stern look her way, but it made her snort. I glanced at Mason, whose eyes were crinkled with laughter and his hand was hiding his broad smile. I ran my hands over my face. *Crap, my face was warm.*

"I bet he tried to sell you on joining. Do you realize how you sound on the phone?" Mason wasn't hiding his grin now.

"What's that supposed to mean? I was being professional like I was doing research for a book." Heat was shooting down my neck and arms.

"Ma bichette, over the phone your voice is...damn sexy. I heard you this morning answering your phone and your business phone voice is... just take my word for it." Mason was now avoiding looking in my eyes. *Was he blushing?* I swallowed.

"I may never talk on the phone at work again." I was at a loss, I had to get this back on track.

"I think the most we could get from that group is if one of them was at the luncheon anyway. I doubt anyone would share unless they were at the Gilded Hornet again." I let out a frustrated sigh.

"What? You think some swingers from Drake's group were at the Hornet?" He was serious now, all trace of the laughter or blushing gone.

I recounted my talk with Ramone the bartender and his account of the table of women sharing intimate details about Pastor Tom's stamina.

"Eeeewwwwwww!" Felicia mimicked putting a finger down her throat. I had to agree, if not so graphically.

"Is there any way you could get a heads up if the same women come back?"

"I can ask Ramone to call me, but the chances are slim they'll come back so soon or even when Ramone is on duty. What're you thinking?"

"I thought maybe I could somehow get them to talk to me. But, you're right. The chances of catching them soon enough for our purposes are slim."

"Guess you'll have to go to a swinger's meeting," Felicia stated matter-of-factly.

"No way, not happening." I blurted out.

"I don't like it either. You were broken into and then if you showed up, no matter how innocently, at one of their meetings, it could threaten the killer. Let me call this guy and see if we can't meet with a few members anonymously *for your book*." Mason's eyes had a wicked glint to them.

I was about to get defensive about the assumption he could do better getting information than I could, then thought about the comments regarding my phone voice.

"Maybe we've enough already, maybe we don't need to follow up with the swingers. Besides, we haven't checked on the contact information for this Cynthia. That might give us something." Yeah, I was grasping at straws. I was more uncomfortable over the Swingers than I imagined I would be.

"Sure, we could do that." Felicia didn't sound convinced.

"If I'm the *swing* vote, I'm good with postponing further investigation on that front." He was chuckling to himself. I groaned.

Chapter Twenty-two

Music night had consisted of primarily helping Felicia practice her songs. I did play a Disney tune on my Clarinet just to get a little practice in. Roulette covered her ears with her paws. I surmised some of the frequencies hurt her ears rather than taking it as an indication of my playing. I knew I was a little out of practice, but I wasn't that bad.

Mason even brought his guitar over and had us singing along to oldies favorites. The image of him playing is burned into my memory. Roulette's walk before lights out was quick as the evening had a chill with a cold front approaching. We finished the night with a round of spicy hot chocolate.

Mason walked me to work again in the morning and was spending time around the Resort, checking out the various shops and the Gilded Hornet in the off chance the lady swingers would be having lunch or something.

I had several meetings and a luncheon to check in on. I wanted to make an appearance and ensure everything was running smoothly, but my presence had caused problems at one function with some people who felt I should be in lock up because of that lovely article.

I was staying in the background as a result.   I checked in with Brad and the chef. We couldn't use the room where Pastor Tom was killed, the crime scene clean-up crew was finished. But, new carpet had to be installed since the crime scene cleaners had cut out the blood-stained and contaminated section of carpet.

The tables were all dressed and table settings placed perfectly with napkins beautifully folded and standing up on each plate. The wait staff was finishing filling water glasses when the doors opened and people began to file in.

This was a local group that provided services to disabled children. When the microphone was turned on, a voice I knew began speaking, I turned and gawked. Tiffany Davidson, the woman who could cost me my job because of her article portraying me as the only possible killer, was speaking to the group.

"Lunch will begin shortly. Please find your seats and make sure your entrée selection card is showing on your plate."   Then she motioned to somebody in the crowd. "Can you bring my notes please, dear?"

I froze. Every drop of blood drained from my body and I swear my lungs collapsed. Brandon was bringing Tiffany her purse. *Dear? When did he become her dear?* He climbed up the side stairs and handed her a file folder. She grabbed his hand, pulled him close and gave him and thorough kiss. They parted and she smoothed her hair and looked directly at me...then winked.

I marched out to the staging area. I couldn't let my feelings show in front of attendees or employees.

"Brad, everything looks good.   Get the meals delivered as fast as you can. Use your cell phone and contact me if you need me. I have to run back to the office." I didn't wait for a reply, but left Brad and speed walked over to the main hotel area. I practically ran into my office, only to find Mason sitting in the guest chair. I stopped as if I'd hit a brick wall.

"I came by to ..." He stopped and his eyebrows jutted up. "They didn't fire you, did they?"

"No, it's not that." Tears formed at the corners of my eyes and threatened to spill over. I began blinking. He grabbed a tissue from my desk dispenser and handed it to me.

"Thanks."   I dabbed at my eyes and took deep breaths. He stood with worry etched on his face.

"Do you want to talk about it?" His strong voice, low and gentle as a caress, nearly had me crying again. I took another deep breath.

"Just saw Brandon...kissing the reporter Tiffany." I flopped into my chair. "Nothing says 'we're over' like giving a deep kiss right in front of you to the person who's trying to ruin your career." I squeaked out.

"Ahh, I see." He remained standing. "I came by so you could join me for lunch at the Gilded Hornet. No doubt you'd rather be alone now."

I nodded, still dabbing my eyes. Mason left without looking back. No doubt the last thing he ever had to deal with in life was a gal mourning her boyfriend and not jumping at his lunch invitation.

How could Brandon move on so easily? That was what really bothered me. How serious could his marriage proposal have been if he could move on so completely in a matter of a few days? Sure, I'd felt he never really knew me or accepted me, but replacing me so fast turned me cold inside. What did that say about me for sticking with him for so long? Geez, this was a mess. My life was a mess. I could blame Tiffany for all of this, and I was working myself up to do just that.

But, Brandon had wanted a completely different person if I was honest. Our last dinner when he botched the whole proposal came back to me in a flash. No, Tiffany was getting revenge for a high school slight she felt. But, truth be told, Brandon wasn't my soul mate and we had grown apart. I still felt betrayed and stabbed in the back. Tossed out. Discarded.

I kicked myself at the memory of Mason's look when he realized I was bawling over Brandon. He had retreated emotionally, shut down, and his eyes reflected that when they lost some of the joie-de-vivre usually present. For all my bluster that he wasn't my type, he did make me feel alive. Something I hadn't felt since mom had died. I had probably damaged even a friendship with Mason.

Trying to throw some reasonable doubt to the police about my being a murderer was stalled out for the moment. I couldn't think about that because my mind went back to the newspaper article...and Tiffany...then that kiss.

I buckled down and got a few more hours of work done with the primary goal of leaving work early. I had definite plans to drown my sorrows at the Gilded Hornet. I checked completing the membership newsletter off my to do list and checked in on several projects in the works. I let Chad know I was finished for the day and was leaving, to which he informed me I looked terrible and should go home and take some Vitamin C. *Great.*

Ramone was on duty when I sat at the polished dark wood bar. The old world décor and elaborate carving on the dark wood throughout the pub usually made me feel like I had transported to Britain, but not this time.

"What's wrong with you Chica?"

"Guy trouble. Give me a double Glenfiddich, the eighteen-year-old stuff." Might as well have the good stuff. I tried to take a gulp, but who was I kidding? I choked and took a few minutes to catch my breath again. I decided to sip it after that.

"You want to talk about it? I don't share with anybody, the sanctity of the confessional and all." Ramone eyed me. It probably wasn't very professional of me to let an employee see me in this shape, but I was beyond caring. Desperate times required...what was it... desperate measures. That was it.

"No thanks, Ramone. But, when I'm done you can get a cab to take me the three blocks home, okay?"

"Sure thing. I got it covered." *Yeah, sure, whatever.*

I was nursing that double scotch and working on a good pity party when Ramone caught my eye. He kept motioning with his chin over to a table behind and to the left of me. I hoped this wasn't anything I needed to handle as management because I was in no shape to do so. I swirled my bar stool around, nearly falling off, to see two nicely dressed middle aged women drinking Martinis. Who goes to an English Pub and has Martinis? When did the bar stools get so tall? Seriously.

"Honey, you doing okay there?" I must have drawn their attention. So much for keeping to myself and wallowing.

"I'm fine. Men just suck, you know." That was as eloquent as I was going to get at the moment.

The two exchanged a look and the blonde with the short perfect hair offered for me to join them at their table. Since I was afraid I couldn't safely get down from my bar stool after another sip or two I figured this was a good plan. They ordered the beer cheese spread and crackers.

"Dear, how can we help? We can listen at least. That helps." Brunette started.

"We've been there, really. What happened? He break your heart?" Blonde finished.

"Men...they...they're... well, he kissed her, right in front of me. Not a peck on the cheek or anything. It was the tonsil hockey all right. And she, that she-devil, she rubbed it in...looked at me and winked, like she had won or something. Who does that? A she-devil does that, is who." They both nodded their encouragement with a look of commiseration in my pain. I realized I may not have made sense enough for them to understand, but it did help to get it out. Sort of.

"Don't get me wrong," I sipped more Scotch and waited for the burn down my throat to stop. "He didn't support me in my dreams, just wanted a little woman to have babies and maybe a sideline job, but not a career. Never a career. Oh, no." I was on a roll, so I took another sip. The Glenfiddich was getting smoother the more I drank.

"Honey, you deserve somebody who'll root for you in your career, who isn't threatened by a strong woman." The brunette lady was getting fired up.

"Then this whole thing with Pastor Tom, it's been horrible, just horrible." I realized too late what I had said and hoped they wouldn't connect me with the blasted article Tiffany wrote.

"Oh, you poor dear. Don't waste your grief on him." The blond was getting into it now. From the sound of this response, maybe they knew him.

"It's just, well he counseled me. Really helped me through a bad time...my mom died and all." Which was true, my mom had died, years ago. Just mentioning her brought tears to my eyes.

"Yeah, helpful, that was Tom." Blond again.

"Oh, did you know him? He was so compassionate... and giving." I hoped I wasn't pouring it on too thick, it was hard for me to tell since I was definitely tipsy now. I smeared beer cheese on a cracker and popped it in my mouth. I needed more on my stomach than scotch.

"Oh yeah, we knew him. But there was another side to him, so don't let his death get you down."

Well, they weren't bad mouthing him, but they sure weren't painting him as a saint either. I glanced over at Ramone behind the bar and he nodded to me. Was it possible these two gals were part of the swingers he'd overheard last week?

"Just the thought of such a good person being killed like that is horrible. You know, in pain and frightened... all alone." I took another sip but made it look like a big swallow. Perhaps the alcohol allowed me to say these things without a mocking tone, rolling my eyes, and gagging.

The two gals were looking at each other, seeming to debate without saying a word. Finally, they focused on me again.

"We knew him, rather well actually. You may not believe us, and he isn't here to defend himself. But, he used women and it sounds like he used you too."

It was hard to tell if they might have been mothers of some girls he had taken an inappropriate interest in, or if they were swingers. Well, only one way to find out at this point.

"I never believed the rumors about him and girls at the church, if that's what you mean. Especially that Cynthia, or whatever her name was. He wasn't like that, he was a man of God." If they believed me, I should get a role in the local theater group.

The blond swallowed and took a breath before she spoke again. "He wasn't exactly as he presented himself." She leaned in and proceeded in a whisper. "We were in the same swingers group." She stopped and scrutinized me. I nodded to encourage her to continue.

"We all knew who he was, and he would use Solomon as an example of God rewarding a righteous man with multiple partners. I didn't care about that, my husband and I had our own reasons for being there." She took a gulp of dark beer and glanced around before continuing.

"I didn't know that my daughter had begun attending his church with her best friend until she confided that he had persuaded her best friend that she was chosen to be with him...as his concubine."

I lost my acting credentials at this point. My mouth was gaping and my eyebrows were up into my hairline.

"What did you do?" My voice had gone up an octave at that.

"I didn't have to do much. My daughter confided in their school counselor and the family moved away suddenly. But, my husband and I changed swinger groups. Another thing, I don't think his wife wanted to participate. That's what another husband told us, he didn't want her as a partner if she wasn't willingly involved."

"Damn." I clamped my hand over my mouth, afraid I had just blown my act. "Sorry, I'm just shocked by all this. By swingers, you mean...umm, swapping and stuff?" Maybe that would cover my reaction.

She cleared her throat and shared another look between her brunette friend before she answered. "All I'm saying is, he wasn't the man everyone thinks he was. Don't take his death too hard." With that, they began gathering their purses to leave.

"Thanks. That couldn't have been easy to tell me. I appreciate it." I held my hand out, I really was hoping for their names. "I'm Bettina. It was nice to meet you." I blurted out. *Bettina? What kind of name was that?* Well under pressure and with roughly two shots of scotch in me, I was lucky I hadn't gone with Maybelline or Lucile.

They gave the names Debbie and Kate but didn't give any last names. When they left, I quickly asked Ramone if there was a last name from their credit card.

"You're in luck. Deborah Patterson paid for the drinks and beer cheese." He had a big grin on his face. The name seemed vaguely familiar.

"Were they part of the swinger's ladies?"

"Yeah, that's what I was signaling you. They were among the group of woman that day, although those two didn't say much about the Padre. Not like a few of the others I told you about." Debbie had said they changed swinger groups, so she was into the lifestyle and was in Pastor Tom's specific group at some point. Could she have put an end to his seducing the young ladies and girls? Maybe it was her daughter and not a friend's she was talking about. The number of people who could easily have been the killer just kept growing. But, I was fairly sure she hadn't attended the luncheon.

"Think one of them killed the guy? The brunette looked like she was disgusted talking about him?" His voice was low but forceful.

"I don't know enough about their interactions with Pastor Tom to say. But they may know something they didn't share with me."

"But, they knew Drake used the girls from the church. Right?" His jaws clenched and his hands were twisting a towel tight, although it didn't appear to be wet at all.

"Not sure about that. Still, doesn't mean they would kill him unless their daughter had gotten hurt."

"It sure seems there were enough people who knew what he was doing and didn't do something for the girls. They should answer for their looking the other way, too."

I let it go without a comment. I was about to order another drink and continue my wallowing over Brandon when Ramone's eyes focused just behind me and I felt a tap on my shoulder. For a second I prayed Chad hadn't found me in the bar getting sloshed after I' left work early. I turned, managing not to fall off the bar stool this time, to find Mason.

"I was concerned when I didn't find you in your office to walk you home." His eyes weren't giving any hint of his mood, and his voice was controlled and even. I had wanted to avoid this, avoid seeing how I'd hurt him with my reaction over Brandon moving on so quickly...with Tiffany.

"I decided to have some drinks and avoid you, for both our sakes." I blurted out while staring at the elaborately carved wood décor on the opposite wall. He took my empty glass from the bar and sniffed.

"Looks like you got a good start. Need more time to drink and avoid me?" I looked at him to find him grinning and his eyes twinkling.

"Honestly, I need food. Another drink and I'll probably regret it tomorrow. But as for avoiding you..." I placed a finger on my lips to stop me. *Gulp*. I wanted to say how I hated I'd upset him, I never meant to hurt him or anything. But, I also knew that I couldn't deny my feelings of betrayal, they were important too.

"How about you and Felicia have dinner at your house and I'll come by later for couch duty? I've something to take care of. Besides, I've a feeling you need to vent with a girlfriend and not worry what you say." He placed my hand on his arm and we walked out.

I told him all about my acting job with Deborah Patterson and her friend Kate as we strolled the few blocks to my house. He nodded but said little. He left after I was safely inside with Felicia promising to be back after a few hours. Was it wrong for me to miss him as soon as I saw him back his car out and drive away? Even when I was upset Brandon had left me in the dust?   *I'm clearly conflicted, or just cursed in relationships.*

Chapter Twenty-three

I had vented my heartbreak with Felicia over dinner but found fewer tears available than before.

"I'm surprised, I want to call him right now and tell him off." She ground out with venom. I had seriously considered doing the same, or maybe a sharply worded text message. A part of me feared I would retract everything if I spoke to him.

"But, I've been thinking that he was never really right for you, you know? I mean, once I got past how he'd become part of the family, I realized there was no deep connection there." When had my flighty cousin gotten such clarity on this topic?

"I thought about it a lot, too. It was a romance that was comfortable. I realized that doesn't mean we cared about the same things in life. I never felt my dreams were his dreams or vice versa." Yep, no deep connection. No foundation for the relationship.

"Can I ask you a sensitive question?" We were on the couch with our legs curled under us and she was unusually serious. I nodded, not sure what was coming next.

"I know you miss your mom, but do you think..." She took a big breath and slowly let it out. "...maybe you have abandonment issues? You were so young when she died, and that makes a lasting impression."

Who was this person and where did my fun-loving cousin go?

"I don't know about that. Why would you even ask such a thing?" *Okaaaaay, maybe I was a little defensive on this topic.*

"Don't bite my head off. I just wondered if...maybe, subconsciously of course....you stayed with Brandon because he was so reliable? The kind of guy who would never leave you." Leave me like my mother did?

"Well, I would've been wrong on that score. He left me after all." I sounded like I'd just won an argument, but I wasn't sure what I was arguing about really. *Could there be something to what she said after all?*

The doorbell broke-up the serious discussion. Felicia jumped up and rushed to the door, waving for me to hide in the kitchen.

She adopted a deeper voice and yelled, "Identify yourself please." I smiled and chuckled. She wasn't fooling anybody.

"It's Delores, quit fooling around."

Felicia looked at me for confirmation. I shooed her away from the door and welcomed Delores in, but she said it would only take a minute. She thrust into my hand a baggie of homemade chocolate covered pretzels. At the holidays she made these for the neighbors.

"I just wanted to drop by and thank you for the card."

"Thank you for your help. I know it wasn't easy"

She nodded and we both shuffled our feet.

"You're looking a little ragged dear. You need to take care of yourself. Don't let all this hubbub get you down." I realized this was our version of patching things up and getting back to normal.

"I'll do that. Thanks again Delores." She turned and walked birdlike down my steps.

I closed the door with a smile on my face. The pretzel snack was gone in under five minutes between us. I helped Felicia practice her songs, which amounted to giving critiques of timing mostly.

Mason was back well before lights out time and I felt awkward with the situation between us, so I went to bed early and read. But, I could hear the two of them talking down stairs. One part of me wanted to eavesdrop and find out what they were discussing, but the other part wanted to avoid any further drama. I went to sleep thinking how complicated my life had suddenly become, thinking about whether my mom's death in my youth was impacting my relationships.

I was back at work early the next day for a breakfast event for a local horse riding therapy charity. I was leaving the conference center where Pastor Tom died walking back to my office in the main hotel. The breakfast was over and everything was being cleared away. My presence hadn't caused any problems and I didn't get stares from the attendees like before.

I took my time and enjoyed the autumn leaves all around me. The resort had lovely landscaping, but the leaves nearly glowed in the sunlight. I breathed deep the crisp air tinged with a hint of moisture. Perhaps the worst was behind me.

Opening the door to my office I saw Detective Lawrence exiting Chad's office. *I guess I spoke too soon.*

Detective Lawrence studied me with a hard look and turned to speak to Chad.

"Please get me that information right away."

"Yes, before I leave today you'll have it." Chad was near groveling. Oh, this wasn't good.

I ducked into my office and closed the door. I spent the next few minutes wringing my hands and struggling to decide what to do next. I decided to confront Chad and hope to find out what information the detective was trying to obtain on me now. I couldn't imagine what more he needed after talking to the staff and my family.

Chad's door was open, but I knocked and waited in the hall regardless.

"Julienne, I don't have time right now. I have a hundred things all due immediately. To think my job used to be done by three people, three. Maybe tomorrow, but I don't see this workload letting up, in fact..." He barely looked at me but kept typing on his computer and complaining.

"Chad, what did the detective want? Was it about me again? Haven't they got anybody else they suspect?" I sounded desperate to my own ears.

"I'm sworn not to discuss this with anybody. I can't comment, really." I started to wring my hands again.

"Look, the membership has quieted down for the moment. Just pray there are no more articles in the paper with you as the villain." He turned back to his computer, I'd been dismissed, so I left before he could pick up his ranting where he left off.

I thought about Tiffany yesterday purposely kissing Brandon and rubbing it in my face. I wouldn't be surprised if she wrote another article to ensure I lost my job.

I slunk into my office. My only option was to keep gathering alternative suspects to turn over to the police. I felt like I had exhausted all the ways I had available... except calling Cynthia's family. I didn't feel comfortable with bothering a grieving family. That was even worse than being recruited for a swinger's group.

I had made a note of the phone number Delores had given me on my phone in case I ever got the nerve to call. I don't know this was the time. I wasn't sure the best way to even start the conversation, but when a woman answered with a lukewarm greeting I took a leap.

"Hello, ma'am. I'm calling from Colorado Springs. If you don't mind, I'd like to ask you a few questions about your daughter Cynthia." I crossed my fingers and held my breath, fully expecting to hear a dial tone next.

"Well, blow me over with a feather. Nobody called when she died. Is it 'cause that piece of pond scum got his just deserts?"

"I heard Pastor Drake knew Cynthia and...was distraught over her death. Perhaps you could share some thoughts for the memorial book we are putting together for his family." I don't know where that came from and how I didn't gag saying it. I was beginning to wonder at my ability to lie so easily.

"Sure, you can put in the memorial book how he got my girl pregnant, then threw her aside like she was trash to be discarded. My sweet girl was devastated and couldn't go on with the shame of believing his lies."

I swallowed. Pastor Drake really had been a piece of work. For a moment I remembered feeling trapped as he grabbed me. My office seemed to close in around me and my stomach clenched. I shook my head and took several breaths before continuing.

"I'm sorry, but your daughter was pregnant? By Pastor Tom? That seems hard to believe." It wasn't that hard to believe, I was just hoping she wouldn't clam up on me. I grabbed a piece of paper and pen to take some notes.

"Well, I sure told that snooty woman who called for my address to send flowers. His secretary, or maybe she just cleaned up his messes. I don't understand how that was kept quiet in that Peyton-place church."

Indeed, how was it kept quiet...and Meredith's story was confirmed, at least in part. Cynthia's mom did tell her, but did she know before that call? Could Meredith have put a permanent end to his using the church girls? Did she slip into the conference center and wait until he was alone? I wrote down those thoughts.

"I'm shocked to hear this, just shocked. Did the elders or his wife know? Surely somebody would've done something." Couldn't hurt to ask.

"Sure, I made Cynthia call the youth director guy. She didn't want to talk with him, she felt so dirty thinking she was specially anointed to be with Pastor, so foolish I was on the other house phone line when she called. He was clearly not going to do anything about it, no matter how much he promised to confront Pastor Drake."

I was writing fast in hopes I could read my chicken scratch later. So, Robert Crandel talked with Cynthia and her mom about her pregnancy.   Did he tell anybody or keep it to himself? Did Pastor Tom hold Crandel's sexual orientation over his head to keep such complaints from going any further?

"What makes you think he wouldn't follow up?"

"He was quick to make the promise, but when I spoke up about wanting Drake exposed to the church and removed from leadership, he backpedaled – saying it wasn't up to him. I thought we should come out and talk to the elders, they had a responsibility to my girl. But he warned me not to, he would call if it was necessary. Never heard from him again." She huffed. I leaned back in my chair, releasing a squeak.

"Ma'am, this is astonishing. No doubt you're upset and I don't blame you. Did you or your husband come out to confront Pastor Drake, maybe after Cynthia passed?"

"No, we didn't. I can't say about her older brother. He took her death rather hard and he's got a temper, that one. He disappeared right after the funeral and we haven't' heard from him again. If he confronted Drake, we would've heard about it though." Her voice became more sullen as she talked.

"Brother huh. What's his name?"

"David."

That didn't help, I wasn't aware of any David that would be the right age. But I felt as though I was missing something,

"I shouldn't bother you any further ma'am. I'm sorry for your loss." I was, too.

She hung up without another word.

I sat for a few minutes considering Meredith. She had shared many things with my neighbor Delores at lunch, but she withheld that Pastor Tom seemed to have gotten a girl pregnant. Perhaps she figured if anybody used the contact information she shared they would find out. I didn't know what to think about Crandel.

I was at a point where I either turned over what I had to the police or got more directly involved. I'd managed to be on the edges without direct involvement...okay, there was the catering undercover gig. But, I hadn't asked questions directly to the "suspects" I had identified. I was considering going to visit the church, Meredith in particular.

I looked up the church phone number and dialed. It was answered on the second ring...by Meredith. I hung up. I had one more work meeting to attend and some paperwork, then I could take a quick drive to the church before the office closed.

Chapter Twenty-four

I had seen car sales lots smaller than the parking lot for the Pastor Tom's church. It had just a handful of cars at the moment, but I had no doubt it was packed on Sundays. I've driven past on Sundays a few times over the years, and they even have a traffic cop to get everyone in and out of the lot, like at big concerts. Except this was every Sunday.

I made my way to the office. It had nice plush carpet, religious themed oil paintings and sculptures decorated the space with a few plants to create a serene setting.

"How may I assist you, young lady." The woman sitting at the wooden desk had lovely salt and pepper hair in a modern short cut, stylish clothes, and perfectly coordinated jewelry.

"Meredith? I'm a neighbor of Delores's. I believe she mentioned me when you had lunch." She looked me up and down and pursed her lips.

"She may have, but I never expected you to have the nerve to come here. You really should leave before somebody sees you and calls the police." She looked out the door behind me.

"I need to talk to you, and the sooner that's done I can be long gone." I tried to appear like I wasn't going to budge.

"Shut the door then and get on with it." I snatched the office door closed. Her jaw was set hard, I could see a jaw muscle clamping. I had to make this fast.

"You knew Cynthia was pregnant, did you tell anyone? Tell the elders? Tell his wife?" I watched her reaction carefully.

Her initial fire that flared quickly, died down. "I knew, and I'll have to answer to the Lord for my part in the whole sordid affair."

"Your part? Can you please elaborate on that?"

"Young lady, I know Delores believes you're innocent of his death, but that doesn't mean I trust you." She ran a shaking hand over her forehead. "It isn't a matter for gossip, this'll hurt the lives of people I care about." She was pale and her hazel eyes overflowed with worry.

"I'm not here for juicy gossip. I know what I've already figured out that there were some *unsavory* actions on Pastor's part. You can't bury it, it'll come out at some point and it could help find the true killer if it's sooner rather than later."

The glass door to the office burst open and in strode Robert Crandel who supposedly also knew Cynthia was pregnant. *Crap, do I confront him now?*

"Meredith dear, the copier has another paper jam." He barely even glanced my way. "I have an appointment with the music director shortly, can you be a dear and run off 200 copies for me." He handed over a manila file folder.

"Sure, I'll get right on it." She looked pointedly at me, but I wasn't done yet. I closed the office door again and faced them both.

He held out his hand. "I'm Robert Crandel, welcome. You are...?"

Oh boy, awkward.

"I'm Julienne." His eyebrows perked upward waiting for my surname. I coughed, "LaMere." I few moments of silence, then.

"Wait, you're that girl from the paper that they suspect in Drake's death." His eyes had gotten big and he swallowed.

"I think it's time we all air a few things. I spoke to Cynthia's mother." I made a split-second decision to jump in with my questions. "You both knew she was pregnant. Want to tell me what either of you did about it, or did you just cover Tom's ass and let that poor girl kill herself?"

They were staring at each other and ignoring me now.

"You knew?" They said in unison. *Interesting.*

"Yeah, it seems momma bear informed both of you. So, what did you do with that information? Time to share now." I had crossed my arms and had my legs apart in a dominating pose, or at least I hoped that was the effect in my pantsuit and pumps.

Crandel nodded his head my way as a question to Meredith.

"She has a vested interest too. If she didn't kill him, then even in death *Pastor* is going to take down another innocent person." Her words dripped with resentment.

"Since when did you stop being his cheerleader? When did you stop covering for him?" Crandel, hands on hips, was starring at Meredith like a strange specimen.

"I was never..." She stopped and tears formed, ready to spill over. "I guess I woke up to the truth. I'd been foolish. A foolish old woman."

Crandel relaxed his stance. "You were sucked in by his charisma like everybody is...at first. You lasted longer than most under his spell, I guess."

I let the scene play out without my interference, hoping to get more from them than bumbling questions on my part.

Meredith wailed, "I loved the bastard. I can't believe I was so blind to what he was doing." The tears began to fall and a sob escaped. She covered her eyes with a hand and collected herself. She grabbed a tissue to wipe the tears.

I couldn't hold myself back any longer.

"What finally happened that you saw Pastor Tom's unsavory side? Must've been something big, I'm guessing." This could be important and I needed her to open up. I crossed my arms and waited.

What little coloring she'd retained now vanished and she appeared a breathing ghost.

"I never believed the rumors, you know. It was unthinkable that he'd take advantage of the teen or college age girls. I mean, he had Sarah for God's sake. But then that Cynthia was always around. Counseling sessions in his office were taking longer than usual. One day...." She halted and swallowed several times, looking between Crandel and myself with pleading eyes. I tapped my foot. "I...I...I didn't know she was in the office. I knocked and walked in and they...they were right there on his desk. I...I was in shock. God forgive me. I never told anyone." She closed her eyes and shook her head, as if trying to get rid of the image.

"She stopped coming around and I thought maybe it was a lapse in judgment, a moment of weakness. Until I over heard the elders and assistant pastor confronting him about *wife swapping*. He actually defended his actions." She blew her nose, squared her shoulders, and steeled herself again. "I can't say I'm sorry he's been removed, perhaps by the hand of God, from any ministry ever again." Her chin jutted up. I could see her killing him, as God's hand naturally. Of course, I absolutely could never risk sharing that thought with Delores.

"Where were you when he was killed? Did you go out to the conference center or hotel at all that day?" It was obligatory to at least ask.

Meredith raised a finely penciled eyebrow. "No, I had no reason to. I had turned in my resignation and didn't want to be around him." She studied me for a heartbeat. "You can't seriously think I'd have killed the swine."

"Can anybody swear they saw you here in the office when he was killed?"

"No, it was a slow day with several staff at the luncheon." She sank back in her ergonomic chair like a rag doll with the stuffing removed.

I spun around to face Crandel, my arms still crossed. "So what's your story? You knew about Cynthia and you apparently didn't have any doubts about Pastor Tom's true character. Did you do something to stop his inappropriate activity with the teen and college girls in the church? They were under your watch and care." I was surprising myself with this newfound assertiveness. I had no idea how long it would last, though.

Now that the spotlight was on him, his hands became restless, like a hummingbird darting here and there, straighten his collar, ran his fingers through his hair, hiked his pants.

"I did confront him like I promised. He...he was vicious. He struck out at me, threatened me. I couldn't do anything... I love this job. I need this job." His voice was strident, pleading. My mind was trying to fill in the blanks. Threatened him, just like I had conjectured. I motioned with a hand to continue.

"So, it's true then. You play for the other team?" I blurted out.

Crandel's adam's apple bobbed as he swallowed then licked his lips. I should've picked up on it sooner myself. He wasn't flaming, definitely subtle, but still right there.

Meredith's eyes widened, but it wasn't the reaction I expected. I raised an eyebrow at her.

"Oh, I suspected. But there've never been complaints of his behavior or ability. In light of what we've just discussed, it seems less important than it would've been even a few months ago."

I turned back to Crandel. "So, he threatened you? Threatened to tell your secret and get you fired, is that accurate?"

"Yes, that sums it up. He knew I'm paying for my mom's nursing care and couldn't afford to lose the job." He moved to the window and stood staring out, his hands finally still, grasping the window frame on either side.

"You were seen outside the building smoking prior to Pastor Tom's murder. Where were you when he was killed?" I shifted my weight and placed my hands on my hips.

"I was still smoking. I knew we were about to eat and had ditched the last bit of my session, so I was in no hurry to get back. And before you ask, I don't remember anybody seeing me when the sessions broke out. Everybody was focused on getting seated for lunch." He was matter of fact, deflated. I could sense his resignation that it was a matter of time before his secret was out and he lost his job.

"I know you both didn't have to talk to me, so I appreciate your sharing. I do have a vested interest. But, I have to warn you, I'll share this information with the police. I only want the police to broaden their search so a killer can be caught." I'd never felt I was good at public speaking, or speeches. But, that was pretty good I thought.

"Oh put a sock in it. You just want off the hook and are happy to put one of us on that hook." Meredith snarled.

Well, there was assertive and then there was just rude.

Chapter Twenty-five

I sped all the way across town and back to work without anybody noticing my absence. That wasn't as comforting as I thought.

I found the report that Claudia had finally compiled detailing which staff had worked the day Pastor Tom was killed slipped under my door. I glanced over it, running down the names, but quickly got an empty manila folder and placed them inside and out of sight for the moment. I tucked the folder with my purse in a drawer so I'd remember to take it home with me.

I was a little late to the resort florist to coordinate floral centerpieces for an upcoming wedding reception. As I speed walked across the open plaza with shops lining the edges, I spotted Crystal. Mason had said she went to Pastor Tom's church and was proud of him. I needed to see how she reacted to me. Hopefully, I'd still be here for awhile and I didn't want working together to be awkward. I would just have to be a little later to meet with the florist.

"Crystal, I'd like to offer my sympathies for your loss. I understand you attended Pastor Drake's church. " I attempted a funeral director's serious yet soothing tone and a sincere look.

Her eyebrow twitched up briefly. "Thanks, Miss LaMere." She turned to leave.

"Do you have a minute to talk? I won't be long." I got out before she could get far. She turned back slowly, a look of long-suffering you expect from a teenager on her face.

"Look, I don't know if I should be talking to you. Aren't you a suspect or something?" *So much for keeping the awkward out of our work relationship.*

"I couldn't say. The police questioned me, but I haven't been arrested or told not to leave town." She didn't think that last part was funny like I intended it. It was all true, I didn't have to tell her I had a lawyer running interference.

"I didn't kill your pastor, which means somebody else did." I just let her think on that...for a few seconds apparently.

"Well, I don't know about that. What do you want, anyway?" I couldn't tell if she was more concerned I wasn't in jail or that somebody else was the killer.

"I wanted to express my sympathies to other staff who attend your church. I thought you might know who else on staff that includes." *Whew, for once it sounded as good spoken as it did in my head. I think.*

"I suppose that's alright. Courtney, Simone, Bryan, Adam, and Bradley are the only ones I know of. It's a big church so I only know the ones around my age." She spun on her heels and took off. If I could only get her to move that fast during clean up after events. I wasn't encouraged by her thinking I was a suspect due for arrest any moment. Never mind that was exactly what I feared.

I took care of the ordering details of items at the floral shop and was back in my office less than an hour later. The many aspects of Pastor Tom's death and the tangled web of his seedy activities were never far from my mind. I wanted to look up Deborah Patterson from the Gilded Hornet yesterday. It was the only connection to the swingers group that I had. At least, I thought she was part of the swingers group. If not, I suspected she knew people in the group.

I checked LinkedIn first and found the name but no picture. She worked for a law firm as a paralegal. It didn't tell me much else. Next, I checked the reliable Facebook. I found her profile with relaxed privacy settings. From the profile picture I could tell it was definitely the same woman I talked to yesterday.

She listed a husband Peter, so I clicked on his profile. The photo seemed a bit familiar even if it showed him running in a t-shirt and shorts. I hadn't expected to recognize him. He was identified as a corporate lawyer employed by a legal publishing company in town.

Well, that was all interesting. Particularly that he seemed familiar. I wish I could place why I felt I knew him from somewhere. This happened sometimes. I dealt with so many people on the job, but also through my family. Aunt Regina exposed me to the musical community with her involvement in the symphony while Uncle Lars owned a gallery in Manitou Springs, the artsy enclave in the adjoining township. Then Porsche hung with a number of academics from Colorado College. It was often hard for me to place where or how I recognized somebody. Could he have attended the luncheon?

I tapped my fingers on the desk. What to do now? How far was I willing to go on this? I had already gone to Pastor Drake's church and confronted two of my prime suspects. But, I was now bordering on stalking a stranger. There just had to be an "in" to talk to one or both of them.

I began looking at the husband's Facebook again. I didn't think the wife had a motive, at least I didn't *think* she did. But a man in the swinger's group might have a beef against the good ole pastor, might have seen how he treated his wife. Which made me think of the reception when I walked in on Widow Drake and a man. I studied the profile photo. There was just no way for me to be sure from the brief glimpse I got at the funeral reception compared to the poor profile photo.

I was hoping for two or three degrees of separation, somebody he knew who knew somebody I knew, somehow. I spent the next hour and a half clicking through his friends and their friends, at least on the people whose security allowed me to do that. It didn't get me anywhere. Only a few of his friends didn't have some level of privacy setup, so I wasn't getting far.

I sat staring at his Facebook page again. There had to be some way to bump into him by design. I clicked on his photo to get a larger view and see the details better. I looked at his t-shirt more closely. The shirt, there was something about the shirt. It was hard to read the words, but it featured a cartoon drawing of a man in green clothes and hat and a bright red beard.

The name came to me like a jack-in-the-box popping up. It was a downtown Irish bar that sponsored a running club. I pumped my fist in the air. *Yes, got it!*

I quickly searched for the running club and found their website. Prominently featured was the same t-shirt, a new release for participants having completed fifty runs. That would mean Peter Patterson was a regular...and they had a run scheduled for tonight. In one hour. I scrambled to shut down for the day and get home. I couldn't run the few blocks home in the shoes I had worn. They were practical enough for a short walk, but I wasn't willing to risk tripping at faster than a power walk. It took me fifteen minutes.

I burst through my front door to find nobody home – no Felicia, no Mason. I tore up the stairs and began searching for my newest Race for the Cure t-shirt and jogging pants. I grabbed a barrette for my hair and was downstairs writing a note explaining where I was going in a record five minutes. I had to sit long enough to slip on my running sneakers and lace them up. I took a few credit cards, ID and car keys so I didn't have to worry about a purse. They were safe in my jogging pants zippered pockets.

I was making good time, but I knew the parking shuffle downtown would be the usual prowling for a space to open. There was a blue truck I'd noticed behind me for awhile, no doubt looking for parking as well. I managed a spot three blocks from the Irish bar and power walked to it; I needed to conserve my running energy. I wasn't a runner by any stretch and I needed just enough running prowess to spot Peter and hopefully catch him when he finished and get him talking. I knew I couldn't keep up with a regular jogger. That was the extent of my plan, I was winging it and hoping to get something from the effort.

I made it with five minutes to spare before the runners were to begin, but it was fairly casual in its approach and many had already begun. I scanned the crowd of fifty or so runners that ranged from young college students up to middle aged professionals and a few new to running, even some moms with baby strollers. But, no sign of the potential swinger hubby.

I found a sign-in station to log your attendance, so you could qualify for the prestigious t-shirts I figured. I approached the young waitress facilitating the event.

"Can you tell me if my running partner has already checked in? Peter Patterson." She glanced through the names.

"He's here, somewhere. Go ahead and sign in yourself." I added my name, well Felicia's anyway. I collected a map of the route through downtown so I could try and head Peter off if he had already begun. I made my way through the crowd and back towards the entrance.

I stopped and looked around, the sensation that I was being watched had come over me. My pulse sped up and I had to keep from giving up and driving home to my safe little cocoon. I scanned the faces in the crowd around me and didn't see anybody that set off alarms in my mind. *Calm down, its nerves from the break in.*

I studied the running route on the little half sheet map and found a way to cut off a few blocks by cutting across a parking lot and hopefully catching up with the early runners. I looked around me one more time and then took off.

My senses seemed heightened, I was aware of the other jogger's pounding feet around me and their voices, every car that passed, the people sharing the sidewalk coming and going from the shops all processed rapid fire in my mind. I couldn't shake the sensation of being watched or maybe followed. My skin crawled.

I saw the parking lot and crossed with the light, but poured on the speed as I wove through the vehicles to cut across. I ducked out of sight behind a big four-wheel drive truck and peeked through the cab windows. Nobody seemed to even notice me, let alone be following. Still, the hair on the back of my neck was standing on end and the hair on my arms was prickling.

I turned and ran hard again through the lot, across an alley, between two brick multi-storied buildings, and emerged on the sidewalk two blocks away. I could see the line of runners in staggered sets, and what might be the object of my mission a block ahead.

He had a fast pace and I doubted I could catch him unless the lights helped me out. I gritted my teeth and picked up my pace again, even though I was already breathing hard. I just barely reached the corner and squeaked across as a car honked its horn at me. I was slightly closer, but he was waiting at the next corner for a light. I slowed up a bit because I was running out of steam. *Just keep running. Where's that infamous second wind?*

But I couldn't keep pace with him. I stopped long enough to check the map and devise another short cut that would put me ahead of him, or maybe even with him considering his pace.

People filtered around me, intent on finishing. It was harder to start back up now that I had stopped. My legs were burning and felt like lead. *Did I mention how I wasn't a runner?*

I began walking again, turned left at the next cross street, then right down two blocks, left for two blocks. The sun was beginning to dip behind Pikes Peak to the West, and bringing twilight. I had managed to get a loping jog going. I was continually looking around, even jogged backwards a few steps. I couldn't seem to shake the feeling of being watched and followed. I finally saw the fast runners a half block ahead, crossing the street right in my path.

When I reached the corner, I was promising myself a drink and food back at the pub. My stomach was beginning to complain as much as my legs, almost. I was wondering if I had missed Peter Patterson when he passed me on the left with an impressive stride.

It was definitely the same guy, Deborah's husband from Facebook. But Facebook was deceptive. The guy was six foot or taller, no wonder he was so freaking fast. My five foot four little legs were no match. In person, I was able to confirm Peter was the man who was holding the recently widowed Sarah at the funeral reception. *Interesting.*

We were closing in on the final few blocks and I kept jogging, but slower and slower. I was down to a power walk when I crossed the threshold into the sponsoring bar again. It was smoke-free by law, which allowed me to try and catch my breath.

The runners who had grabbed seats were high-fiving, clearly on the notorious runner's high, ratcheting the noise level up as well. I slumped into a wooden chair at the closest table and tried to locate Peter while I caught my breath. *Geez, this was supposed to be good for you?* Tantalizing smells reached me and my stomach let loose a loud growl.

The lights were still turned up so I could look around easily. I spotted my elusive prey in a small booth with high backs, alone. For all his suspected social swinger's lifestyle, he was appearing a bit anti-social in this setting. Of course, I had leapt to the conclusion that he was a swinger since his wife knew Pastor Tom and dropped the hint of swingers.

I painfully stood up, my joints already freeing up, so I could force my company on the poor man when a tap on my shoulder made me yelp and jump.

I whirled around to find my face in Mason's chest... well, my nose brushed his soft button down shirt and I could feel the heat radiating off him while his distinctive sensual spicy cologne enveloped me. I couldn't tell if my knees were wobbly because of the run or the proximity to Mason.

"Got your note. Didn't realize you were into running." He looked me over while I was still breathing heavy, not entirely from the running at this point – but I wasn't going to clarify. "Something tells me you aren't all that into it now."

"Wise ass," I muttered.   He chuckled, his eyes sparkling. I shared who Peter was in as few of words possible because I was still a little oxygen deprived.

"What's the plan?" He asked.

"I don't need no stinking plan." With that, I pushed through a few people milling around and plopped down at the booth with Peter, Mason sitting down next to me.

"You don't mind if we join you, do you?" I went for cheery and over confident.

"Thanks, bud. We appreciate it." Mason chimed in, winging it along with me.

Peter's eyebrows furrowed and he stared at us. We had clearly taken him by surprise.

Mason waved a waitress over and ordered Guinness for him and a pale ale for me. He offered to buy Peter a beer but got a shake of the head no.

"I see from your t-shirt you're a regular. This is my first time. Got any advice for me?" He wore the same shirt as his profile picture. I had to get him talking somehow.

"You're pushy... and don't assume I'm alone for long. I'm saving a seat." Well, he sure told me. It was looking like he would be a challenge to get to talk.   Mason stood.

"Sorry, we were just trying to get to know some of the regulars since she's taking up running. No harm." He quickly grabbed the adjoining booth to Peter's back and waved for me to sit down.

"I think this is better. We might learn more if we just watch and listen." That was fine by me. Besides, it sounded like he was expecting company. That might reveal something as well. My stomach let out another growl, even louder than the previous one.

"Cross our fingers," I added. Our beers came and I ordered an appetizer. It occurred to me that this was almost a date, just the two of us...staking out a swinger in a bar. That's a phrase I never thought would ever come up in my life.

I didn't want to share my day yet. I wasn't sure how everything would go over since I went to the church without telling anybody.

They were setting up for the live Irish music. I had heard of the raucous fun, patrons singing along as the guy played on his guitar. They even provide out a song sheet with the lyrics so nobody had an excuse, or so I have been told.

I was beginning to worry that this idea would be a bust when the widow Sarah Drake walked past us and sat down with Peter Patterson. Aha! I wasn't sure what it meant though.

Mason had seen her arrive and craned his neck around to peek in the booth quickly, making it appear he was looking for somebody in the crowd. He even waved to nobody in particular for show.

He looked back at me and raised his eyebrows. He leaned over the table and I met him halfway on my elbows leaning over my beer.

"What do you think of that?" He asked.

"Maybe we've found Drake's swinger group after all. But I don't know why she would be meeting with him now that Drake is dead. Unless she was more of a willing participant than we thought."

"I wonder. I never bought into the whole "no jealousy" or messy emotions thing." He said. Good to know.

"What if Pastor's wife got the emotional support and nurturing she needed from another man? What if they developed feelings for each other? That would give this swinger dude or his wife a huge reason to get rid of Drake." He said. Our heads were so close together I could smell his shampoo. Nice, it blended with his cologne.

"I think, well...Peter could've told Deb some of the initial pillow talk about how Sarah didn't want to participate, and that might have colored Deborah's view of Tom. Since the church elders confronted Pastor and Sarah was going to leave him, I think she wasn't a willing participant. But, I doubt Deb realized her husband's sympathy turned to something deeper." That was my theory of how it happened.

We looked into each other's eyes and I couldn't think of another thing to say. They were a hypnotic hazel, green with golden highlights. I sat back and broke the spell. I felt like I was walking a tightrope strung between two skyscrapers without a safety net when I was close to Mason. It was both scary and exhilarating.

I waved him to lean in and we met over our beers again. I ignored the desire to kiss him or weave my fingers through his wavy hair.

"I want to talk to them, get them to tell us what their story is," I whispered in his ear.

"No. No way. A love triangle is very dangerous and they're near the top of my suspect list. One or both of them could be the killer." He had captured one of my hands and shifted to look me in the eyes. "I don't want you taking any risks. Please."

I promised him before I knew the words flew out of my mouth. He had some sort of magic power. When I first met him I was immune, but he wove a spell like a web spun around me, one strand at a time, weakening my resistance with each new thread. I tried to mentally resolve to break free. It was for the best.

I sat back again but was restless now. I missed his touch when he held my hand. I had to stay focused, so I leaned out of the booth and peeked at Peter and Sarah, the two unlikely swingers who found each other? They were talking, no touching, no heads together, no longing looks, no smiles or blushes. If anything they seemed uncomfortable and stiff. I sat back and just a few minutes later the widow Sarah Drake walked past us with no coat. Bathroom?

"Bathroom break," I stated as I jumped up and followed her. Mason would be mad, but I wasn't planning on any risky tactics. Women go the bathroom all the time and chat.

The bathroom was nice for a bar. The wallpaper was fashioned after antique newspaper that battered fried fish used to be wrapped in. Dark polished wood accents and old fashioned wall sconces completed the décor.

I didn't see her but one of the dark polished wood stalls was occupied, so I began cleaning up with a wet towel from the run. I had been anxious to clean up ever since Mason arrived. I was washing my neck and arms with wet towels when Sarah Drake came out of a stall.

I first noticed her perfect hair with professional highlights seemed a bit scraggly, followed by her manicured hands were sporting ragged nails as if she had been biting them. Her designer clothes in muted hues were impeccable though.

"Not a runner I gather?" I had to get the conversation started and this was an obvious opening topic.

"No, not me. But I applaud your efforts." Her eyes were slightly red and dull, no spark and her voice monotone. As if she were but a shell of a person.

"My first time. I'm going to give it a try, stick with it for a few weeks. See if it gets easier." She was freshening her makeup. I wasn't getting anywhere.

"If you don't mind my saying, it's surprisingly therapeutic. I didn't think it would be." She looked at my reflection in the mirror with an eyebrow raised. I had to get her attention somehow. "You look terribly sad like life has kicked you and you're down for the count. I couldn't help noticing."

"Well, I do mind."

"I get it, really I do. I broke up with my long term boyfriend when he was proposing marriage to me." I let out a heavy sigh, not entirely acting. "Problem was he had mapped out the rest of my life for me, and...well, I hadn't agreed to any of it. He knew what I wanted in life, what was important to me, what fed my soul. He hadn't honored any of my feelings or dreams in all his planning." I wet my paper towel again and let silence take over.

"I can relate. You think you're on the same page, working as a team and devoted partners when you realize he doesn't even see you. You're just the window dressing for his life, the public face. Then he's dragging you down a road you never wanted. Was your's a smooth talker?" Her voice was quiet, matter-of-fact, dry as toast as it ground out the litany. I suspected she had cried the well of emotion dry.

Smooth-talker wasn't a term I'd ever associate with Brandon. "Charismatic in his own way. In the beginning, he made me feel safe, special like the world was right when I was with him. But, I was kidding myself. Before I knew it, a year had passed and I couldn't imagine facing the future without him. Only hours after our breakup, I saw him kissing another woman." My eyes had welled up and my voice was getting rougher. I swiped at my eyes.

"Didn't I see you out there with a guy?" Well, wasn't she observant?

My mind was racing for what to say when I heard myself answer. "Ever have a guy show up unexpectedly in your life who just makes you feel alive again? Who terrifies you for who he is and yet makes you feel wanted and appreciated at the same time?" My voice was soft, a stage whisper. I watched her in the mirror.

She shifted her weight, lifted a hand and placed two fingers against her lips as if she was subconsciously trying to stay quiet. "I believe I know what you mean. What're you going to do?" What a loaded question?

"About the betrayal of him kissing another woman or the surprise man?"

She shrugged a shoulder.

"When I saw him kiss that woman, there was a part of me that hurt so badly I wanted to hurt him back." I watched her closely in the mirror. She bit her lower lip, smearing the newly applied lipstick.

"The heat of the moment passed, but the gut wrenching anguish took over. Maybe I'd like him to feel the pain I'm suffering through. First being treated like a bit part in the movie of his life, nearly invisible and apparently easily discarded...or worse, interchangeable." I hoped that wasn't too obvious. I didn't really feel all this, much.

Her eyes had welled up and a single tear slid down her cheek.

She didn't move when she spoke, staring into the mirror. "But, what can we do, really? We can't lash out and make them hurt, that's wrong. And we're just women. The little women. The unimportant, inconsequential women." Another tear followed the track of the first, but she wasn't angry. Despair was all over her face and in the slump of her shoulders, but no rage that would have triggered a stabbing. At least, I didn't think so. Unless she had gotten any rage out already. She paused, took a slow breath and continued.

"Of course the surprise man makes me feel good, noticed, singularly important. It would be easy to run to him, revel in being desired and valued. Maybe even show the bastard what he's missing..." Another pause, shorter this time.

"But it wouldn't be fair to the man who has been kind and tender, been such a surprise blessing." She choked out with a coarse voice, more to herself.

"And it's dangerous. I see it on the news all the time, jealousy leads to violence. Two men fighting over one woman isn't as romantic as the movies make it seem. As wonderful as the surprise man is, he's upset for my sake, for how I was misused." I said, hoping she would share more and let something slip.

Okay, I took some liberties in the story. I didn't think for a minute that Brandon had misused me per say. I wanted to see her reaction to the hint that she was in a volatile love triangle.

Her pinched eyes studied me, no more tears. For a second I thought she realized I wasn't just a random woman in the bathroom.

"So what do you do?" She managed.

"I can only tell you what I know. The one man isn't worth my tears. I can't let him hurt me any further or take any more of my life. I have to forge a new life for myself."

"What about the man who makes you feel important and special again?" I thought there was a tinge of hope, or perhaps longing in her voice.

"I want to take my time. Be sure he knows what he wants, too. There has to be more than the flash-in-the-pan. I don't have to decide right now." I waited a few heartbeats. "What about you? How's it working out for you?" I held my breath, hoping I hadn't pushed too much.

She opened her mouth to answer when the door opened and two girls in skinny jeans and tight mid-drift shirts invaded the small bathroom.

Widow Drake blinked several times, gathered her purse, flashed me a tight smile and bolted out the door like a startled deer. I waited a minute before exiting the powder room myself.

When I passed Peter's table Sarah and her jacket and purse were gone. I risked another look to find Peter with his hands over his face. He was repeating over and over, "I didn't touch the swine. I never touched him." I guess my talk rattled her. Did this clear her and implicate lover boy?

I quickly shared the highlights of my chat with Mason. We didn't stay any longer and exited as the singing began. If the first song was any indication, these sing-alongs were quite the party. Mason and I left quickly, he had already paid our bill while I was talking with Sarah.

I was a little chilled in my t-shirt now that the sun had set. I was exhausted and after the sips of beer, I just wanted the comfort of sleep. We were quiet as Mason walked me the three blocks to my car. Companionable silence would've been nice, but I was already wondering how I could confess about the rest of my day without getting a frown, or worse.

I was absorbed in my thoughts, but I still noticed the same blue truck from a few hours prior when I first came downtown and was looking for a parking space. It drove slowly past, but I couldn't see through the darkened windows at who was driving.

Mason avoided the usual awkwardness at the car when it seems natural to kiss. He opened the door politely, had me promise to drive directly home and he would be following shortly.

On the way home, I swore the same blue truck was following me. I gave up trying to tell myself I was imagining things, when it pulled up next to me at a light on the right and the driver was wearing a ski mask and pointed his fingers like a gun at me, pulling the imaginary trigger.

I ran the red light, looking in the rear view for a license plate, only it had been removed. I didn't see that truck again on the way home. I took a circuitous route just in case I was being followed. It could've been a prank. I had no real indication that it was more than a random harassment; somebody thinking it was funny to scare a woman alone. But I felt deep down it was connected.

I was never so grateful for my garage before. My hands were shaking on my steering wheel. Felicia was waiting for me with Roulette dancing a welcome at the door from the garage to the kitchen. It was nice to arrive home to lights blazing. When Mason pulled up across the street and pulled into his garage, I knew he'd be over soon and I finally began to breathe again.

Chapter Twenty-six

It was a slow day at work, most of the employees were off with just a skeleton crew on duty at the hotel and restaurants. Chad took the day off to see the fall colors. He always waited a week or so too long to go. The mountains were the best color, but they turned earlier than down here at the mere six thousand seven hundred foot elevations.

I was happy he wasn't a hunter. A prior boss thought it was hilarious to go into gory details about shooting the deer and the entire process of field dressing it. I lost my lunch on his desk one year, I was the one laughing then.

I was in a somber mood sitting at my desk. I'd come clean last night with Felicia and Mason about my confronting Meredith and Crandel at the church. They both were worried I had taken a risk and I hated to cause them worry. I shared that I saw the same truck a few times, but I withheld any reference to feeling followed during the run or the person in a ski mask at the traffic light.

Was the timing of the masked man a few hours after I confronted Meredith and Crandel just coincidence? I didn't think it could be either of them in the mask, but one of them could've recruited a friend to scare me. What about Swinging Peter Patterson and Sarah Drake, had she realized I wasn't just a chat in the powder room?

I leaned back in my chair and stared at the ceiling. My head swam when I reviewed the people who had motive. How could the police even consider me when there were far more viable and likely people in Pastor Tom's life? Oh sure, it was a small time frame to kill the guy. That only meant somebody seized the opportunity or had planned it ahead of time.

I rallied myself and was going through my hundred twenty-two emails and answering the routine ones. It was an hour and a half later when I finally got around to the email from the local leadership foundation that had coordinated the deadly leadership luncheon. It was a formal request for a review of their invoice. Something about a discrepancy in the billing, they claimed fewer people attended than the kitchen charged. They included a list of registered attendees. I smiled and blessed the billing gods for handing me this list.

I was reading through the seventy-five names, looking for suspects. The only surprise, to me anyway, was that Peter Patterson was listed. It was a volatile situation and the scenario I spun for widow Drake wasn't far fetched.

Of course, this list was only good if nobody else entered the conference room facility, such as by the back. I put the list in the file folder with the list of employees who were working the event that day. I looked through those names briefly. I would take them home and look them through again. I had a nagging feeling I was missing something.

I couldn't justify waiting much longer to hand what I had developed as alternative suspects over to the police. Anything further really would be investigating on my own, and that would probably only make my case look worse to the authorities.

My cell phone rang. I was discouraged to see it was my lawyer. Was it bad luck to hear from him?

"Miss, I wanted to let you know that the police have been stubborn in releasing reports of evidence. It can be partially because you aren't charged or been taken into custody, but I would like to be prepared, they might be building a case against you. We should meet to go over your options so you aren't blindsided." I paced in my compact office.

I decided I should share all the viable suspects that existed and the modest details I had cobbled together. I briefed the lawyer what I had gathered so far.

"Perhaps if you, as a lawyer presented the findings to the police, they would take them more seriously than if I delivered them. I don't want all this work to be tossed in the trash." I was proud I had latched onto the idea to have my lawyer handed it to the police.

"I can certainly look over what you have and see if there is anything worthwhile and how to handle it." He probably was dismissing what I had as barely noteworthy. I certainly hoped I could prove him wrong. My future may depend upon it.

We agreed to meet after work at his office. After hanging up I sat rubbing my temples, trying to ease the headache building. I had begun to think I may not be of interest to the police, but the detective was visiting Chad just yesterday and now my lawyer wants to be prepared for charges.

I started going through my notes and files. I wanted to type up a summary so everything was nicely organized to hand over later. I began typing on the computer with a section for each suspect.

I flipped through the papers in the notebook and file folder where I'd collected printouts. I hadn't taken the time previously to look at Claudia's report of employees who worked the luncheon. I glanced over the list, not that many worked the event. I skimmed over Brad's name, but stopped and considered his full name. I didn't know Bradley was his middle name, David his first. Crystal had said he went to Drake's church as well. I placed the employee listing in my file on top along with the printout I finally got from the luncheon organizer on who registered for the event.

I was typing away, getting my thoughts on the various suspects down before I added details. I included a section on the Swinger's group and Seattle Cynthia, even though I didn't have as much to report on those two.

The phone rang and I jumped. I'd begun to feel isolated since it was so quiet in the administration offices. It was one of the retail shops with a member discount problem. Normally, Chad would handle this member question, but I was covering for him. This was one of the first things I trained on, so I felt I could handle it by myself. I tried to handle it over the phone, but it was a new member and I suspected his information hadn't made its way to the shops.

I had to go down to the specialty shop and handle it. I left my notes out but locked my office. I'd only be ten or fifteen minutes even with the walking. After the run yesterday I was too sore for much past a moderate walking pace.

It took me twenty-five minutes before I was back at my office. The door stood ajar, but not enough for me to see if the room was empty or not. I remembered several days ago when my door had been unlocked after I swore I had secured it. Somebody was getting past my lock. Other than some sensitive membership files, I couldn't imagine why anybody would trouble with picking the lock...or however my lock was bypassed.

I decided to walk in like I hadn't noticed and find out if anyone was there. When I barged in, attempting a busy air, I found Brad standing behind my desk reading the notes I had on my computer screen and the file with my notes and printouts had been moved.

"Brad, is there something I can help you with?" The hair on the back of my neck was standing up, even the tiny hair on my arms was electrified. He licked his lips, and his eyes flickered to the door and back to me.

"I know it's a slow day, but I'm still here to help." *That's right, I'm oblivious to your busting into my office and reading confidential information. Well, confidential to me, anyway.* Somehow I sensed the need to get him out of the office and believing everything was fine. No conscious thought, just instinct, spidey sense, whatever.

It was eerie how he just stood there, his eyes roaming. My mind told me he was scheming – but I couldn't entertain that thought.

The musical ring of the desk phone made me jump. It was close to where I stood so I grabbed for it, perhaps a little too quickly. I kept my gaze on Brad.

"Colorado Springs Resort, This is Julienne, how may I help you?" Only silence answered me. After a few heartbeats, I heard the line disconnect and a dial tone droned in my ear. I hung the receiver up.

"Brad, if you don't have something for me I need to get back to work. I'm trying to catch up today." His eyes narrowed slightly, but he slowly moved from behind my desk and past me, out the door.

"Yeah, I need to get back too. Just wanted to say hi."

I smiled and nodded my head.

Once he was out of sight, I quickly closed the door and grabbed a wedge doorstop and crammed it underneath. If the lock wouldn't keep him out, maybe that would.

I wondered why he forced entry into my office because I knew I locked up before I left. What did he think he would find? I glanced over the summary I was composing and the items in the file folder. My eyes stopped at his name on the luncheon staff. David Bradley Folgrath. Could he be...no, that wasn't possible. Or was it? Could Seattle Cynthia's angry brother David be Brad?

I collapsed into my office chair. Brad was new to us, joined us only two months ago. Brad had been at the luncheon with me, setting up the buffet table. So he had access, and from his behavior just now I suspected he'd have the fortitude to stab somebody through with a swordfish. Plus, he had driven me home right after the murder, so he knew where I lived. But motive rested entirely on his being Cynthia's brother. That was just conjecture. At no point did I have Cynthia's last name, which I was kicking myself for now. I couldn't think of any other reason he would be in my office, clearly having by-passed the lock.

I dialed Claudia's extension in hopes of her reading his application to me. I hoped to find out if he listed an address or emergency contact in Seattle. No answer.

I tried to think carefully of the few minutes before and after the murder. Brad and I were checking the buffet setup and I asked Brad to get several crab cracker tools. He had just left when Pastor Tom assaulted me, taking up maybe three to five minutes. Then I left the room.

Could he have returned to find the Pastor drunk and he seized on the opportunity to confront Drake? No, no time for a confrontation, the killer had to be decisive and strike immediately. I couldn't remember when I returned to the room after the clatter of dishes that Anete dropped if the Crab Shell Cracker tools were on the table or not.

Anete! What if she had entered the room from the staging area and passed Brad coming back to the staging area? She would be the only witness to who was in the room. No wonder she was so nervous when I encountered her the next morning walking around the lake. That would explain why she was killed as well. I imagine she was afraid to tell the police since she was here on a work visa.

I didn't like this. First, I hated suspecting an employee I worked along side. Secondly, if Brad was Cynthia's brother and he'd attended the church to get close and keep tabs on the man, waiting for his chance, then he was more dangerous than just anger management issues, more like a cold blooded, calculated killer.

This was wild speculation and I had no way to prove it since I didn't have the resources to determine if he was Cynthia's brother. But, my instinct screamed he was dangerous. He had no reason at all to be in my office.

What about the phone call when I got back with only silence? The timing was suspicious. Could the call have been intended for him, knowing he was in my office, maybe even warning him I was returning? I was getting paranoid now.

Then another thought occurred to me. Brad went to Drake's church and the bulk of my alternate suspects were from the church: the widow, gay youth minister, drunken radio partner, and disillusioned secretary. What if he was assisting one of them by keeping an eye on me? He could think he was helping any one of them by monitoring what I pieced together.

Other than yesterday with my talk to Crandel and Meredith, or my joining the downtown running club with Peter Patterson, why would anybody take an interest in me? Except that blasted newspaper article Tiffany had written. If Brad was assisting one of the church suspects, he'd find a way into my office...and maybe follow me.

I wondered what sort of vehicle Brad drove. Was it a truck like the one that seemed to follow me last night? Was it Brad at the stop light? I shivered as dread spread through my body.

I called Mason, but it went to voicemail. I left him a message that would no doubt seem crazy trying to explain Brad in my office when I know I had locked it. I was hoping he'd come to my office when I was done for the day. I was shaken that the lock on my office was useless.

The day wound down, a slow march towards quitting time, and I still hadn't heard back from Mason. I jumped at every noise and I kept imagining the doorknob was turning like in some B horror movie. I was rattled, but quickly finished the summary document I had started, emailed a copy to myself and printed a copy to give Mr. Chalmers, Esquire later. I tried to get some actual work done, but I knew I would need to go over anything I had done and catch my mistakes tomorrow.

Finally, it was time to go, I took the file for Mr. Chalmers to deliver to the police with me and locked up my office. Although, I wondered how much good locks did lately.

Since I hadn't heard from Mason and he wasn't here, my plan was to power walk the few blocks home. Who was I kidding, I probably would run home. I tore out of the main building without incident and felt I was suffering from the stress and perhaps there was a logical explanation for Brad's actions. *Yeah, right.*

I crossed the street nearly running in front of the Convention Center where the luncheon had taken place nearly two weeks ago now. Although I had been inside since I shivered thinking of Pastor Tom speared through. Perhaps he wasn't a model Good Shepard, and he should have faced charges for his activities if he did take advantage of any under-aged girls, he didn't deserve the horrible death he suffered.

My thoughts made my feet scurry faster and a little chill ran down my spine. I was focused on getting home and being done with my part in this drama when an arm circled my throat jerking me backward and another wrapped around my chest. I couldn't scream and my feet scrabbled for traction to no avail.

Chapter Twenty-seven

I was being dragged into the Convention Center. I clawed at the arm around my throat, more to scream than get air. But it was impossible.

The doors to the Convention Center opened and I was dragged inside, fighting all the way with little effect. My brain registered there was another person besides the one with his arm around my throat. I wasn't processing much past survival in the moment, but the fact of two people stood out to me. My chances of escape had just plummeted.

I was released with a shove into the same room Drake was killed in, only partitioned into a smaller area to isolate this section until the cleanup was complete and the rug replaced. But, this was the spot where the buffet table had been stationed...and the body had been impaled on an icy Swordfish nose. The bloodstain was still on the carpet. I spun around to run for the door but found it blocked...by Ramone. His lips snarled and eyes full of fire.

I gasped. *Ramone?*. I turned to run to the prep area, the only other exit out of the room. But, Brad was between the door and me. Adrenalin was rushing and I needed to fight or run. Run was upper most in my thoughts. My mind was tumbling over itself to think of a way out. They blocked the only exits, so I was reverting to an alternate theory, get them talking.

"Brad, Ramone, what the hell are you doing? You're scaring me. This is unacceptable behavior." Not that I really thought either of them gave a fig anymore, but it always worked for my dad.

"Cut the acting." " Ramone ground out.

"You had me guessing earlier, but not now. At first, I thought your digging up the truth about the church leadership and Drake's hypocritical legacy would cloud the issue, give the police more distractions." Brad...or rather David Bradley said.

My thoughts from earlier came back to me. With the time limit he could've come back to deliver the crab cracker tools, took advantage of Drake's drunk and doubled over state in a split second, and on his way out past Anete.

"You killed him, didn't you? You returned with those crab-leg cracking tools and grabbed your opportunity for revenge before it slipped away." I had put the final pieces together, finally.

David Bradley shrugged, but Ramone surprised me.

"Drake had to pay. Our sisters deserved better than his hands on them." The rage bubbling up made a vein on his forehead pulse. His hands were white-knuckled fists.

Brad jumped in, "It didn't start out that way. I saw what he did to you. I confronted him. Told him I was Cynthia's brother and then hit him with my fist in his smug face.   He slammed into the table and the Swordfish jumped off its stand. We began to wrestle when he lunged at me and I shoved him, he fell into the sword-end. As if God directed that ice sculpture with his very own hand." His monotone voice showed no remorse or even shock. Brad, or should I say *David* Bradley, had a touch of madness to his eyes. You know the look, seeing through another lens that isn't this side of sane.

I bet they fought all right, but when the Swordfish was dislodged I suspect he purposely shoved him onto the sword tip all the way to the head of the fish. That was no accident. Nope, not possible.

David Bradley was to my left blocking the back staging area door and Ramone was to my right where the hallway and exit could be reached. I tried to keep them both in front of me.

"But you just had to drag Cynthia into it, didn't you? I was avenging her just as Absalom avenged his sister Tamar in the Bible. But I won't have her name ruined any further. You were going to expose her weakness – her sin - all over again."

"Okay, I get it. Avenge what he did to her." I wasn't going to admit that I was fuzzy on the whole Absalom and Tamar thing. At this point, I didn't think it was necessary to know either.

"You broke into my house a few nights ago and left that note?" I directed the question at *David* Bradley since he had driven me home the day of the murder he knew where I lived.

"We both did." Ramone volunteered. I was tempted to ask which one of them decided to take my identification badge and frame me, but I had a more urgent question.

"Why kill Anete?" I had a theory, but I was keeping them talking more than anything.

"I took care of her. She knew too much and I couldn't trust her to keep her mouth shut." Ramone shared as if he were discussing a troublesome ant.

Okay, I was wrong. I thought maybe she had tried to black mail them, but she just knew David Bradley had been in the room before she arrived. The phone call Anete complained about Brad getting must have been from Ramone – probably urging this was the perfect opportunity, maybe she heard some of the conversation if the phone volume was turned up.

"Following you in the stupid downtown jogging club was Ramone." David offered.

"Was it you at the stop light trying to scare me?" He didn't answer, only smirked. I was sure it had been him in that dark blue truck that had followed me last night, purposely frightening me at the stop light.

Ramone finally spoke up. "I hung around long enough to see the grieving widow meet with her lover. But you knew about them, didn't you?"

"Yes, I had pretty well figured out their... relationship. But I don't know about your sister." Now that I was thinking of it, Ramone had tried to lead me to the Swingers group all along. Likely to draw attention away from his own involvement in the murder or maybe make me look more suspicious.

I glanced between David Bradley and Ramone, each having killed a person with no hint of a conscience. *They plan on killing me.* The reality of that fact hit me.

At that moment, my cell phone in my purse slung over my shoulder rang. I knew it was Mason wondering where in the heck I was. My mind had been on the meeting with the lawyer and I had mistakenly thought I could hurry and be home before anybody could notice me. I ignored it.

"My sister Carmen. Drake convinced her that a godly man could have many women, like Solomon and David. Same as he told Cynthia. The man didn't deserve to live." I watched him as he spoke. There was plenty of anger, but he seemed rational. Too rational.

"You can still make him pay, guys. Even after he's dead, you can still make him hurt. I can help you."

Ramone smirked. "He had to die, the only way to stop a predator like him. He's already paid with his life, how can he pay after death? Only God can do that."

Well, talk about stealing my thunder. How to follow a statement like that?

"Right now his legacy is that of a great man of God, cut down before he could finish his work. But, if his deplorable actions were exposed to the world, he would be known for the horrible man he was. I can blow the lid off what he did to your sisters. But this isn't the way." Sure, I was grabbing at straws.

"No, We have plans for you." David Bradley said. "You're going to kill yourself from the guilt of...well, killing a respected pastor. We have your goodbye note, typed and printed from your computer in your office. Then the police will wrap this up." I hoped I'd live to get a better lock on my office door.

David Bradley took out a small bottle and shook it like a rattle. "Sleeping pills for you, 'cause everybody knows poison is a girl's preferred way to die. Sorry." My stomach clenched while a shot of cold fear speared through my body. I wondered if Cynthia had taken pills, the thought just popped into my head.

"So, you don't care that Pastor Tom will live on as a virtuous man after what he did to Cynthia and Carmen? You'd rather kill me. I didn't do anything to either of you or your sisters."

I was looking at David Bradley, infusing my voice with the reasonable tone my mother would use when trying to get me to see things her way. I had given up on Ramone, it was clear I hadn't really known him.

"She's got a point." David Bradley looked at Ramone.

"No. She exposes the Pastor and she exposes our part in his death. It's that simple. " He took a step towards me and I backed away from both of them.

"Hey, I'm a victim of Pastor Tom's too. He assaulted me. It's not avenging his victims to kill me." *Made perfect sense to me.*

My phone started ringing again.

"Give me the phone." Ramone held his hand out. Now, why would I give it to him? Maybe I could get to the pepper spray in my purse that Mason insisted I start carrying. It was worth a try, maybe I could even spray both of them.

I reached in my purse, my hand fishing around, fumbling. I seized the spray can and with my thumb popped off the top as I pulled it out. I could feel the nozzle etching where to put my finger so it was pointed away from my face. I sprayed at David Bradley since he was closest to me. For an instant or two, I thought it didn't work. What would I do now? I had no plan B, I was winging this.

His eyes closed then his face began to turn bright red and swell, and he began cursing and yelling. The yelling stopped and he started coughing. I'd been staring at him, but I whirled around and pointed the canister at Ramone.

"I'm walking out, Ramone. Let me go and we can forget you were involved." Okay, that last part was a huge lie to help me escape. I wasn't above lying given the circumstances.

His eyes weren't giving me any clues about his intentions, so I couldn't tell what move he was planning. I noticed the door behind Ramone to the main hallway open and Mason ducked his head inside then back out. *Hey, where did he go?* I tried not to look in that direction. I focused on Ramone.

"Look, you should really help your friend there. Just let me go okay?" Ramone's eyes had a calculating glint and I knew in that moment he was never going to let me leave alive. I think he was the little voice pushing for Pastor Tom's murder. David Bradley may have shoved him onto the sword, but I suspected that Ramone shoved him into doing it. Subtle and subversive, but culpable in my book.

Before Ramone had a chance to answer, or even move, Mason ran into the room and stopped before me, shielding me. He had the wicked retractable nightstick fully extended in his right hand and I still had my pepper spray. It wasn't over yet, but the odds had changed.

"The police are on the way. Get down on the floor." Mason shouted, channeling his inner drill sergeant. Relief flooded me that authorities would be here any second.

David Bradley was doubled over coughing and trying to breathe, he dropped to the floor and continued coughing.   Ramone was getting a frantic look in his eyes, glancing at David Bradley and then at us.

Ramone charged and launched a punch at Mason's head, which he dodged. I moved a few steps closer to the door, but couldn't leave Mason in the middle of a fight. Ramone swung around, crouched and ran in for a tackle, but Mason managed to side-step. Mason spun around and clipped him with the baton on his leg tripping him. Mason followed by pinning him to the floor, somehow he flipped him onto his stomach and had his hands pinned to his back.

"Look, I only phoned David that Drake was drunk and headed back to the Convention Center. I didn't know he was going to kill him." Ramone confessed to being an accomplice to Mason. I planned on telling the police how I saw him influence an unstable David Bradley, admitted he killed Anete, and was party to breaking into my house.

"I'm sure the police'll take that into consideration." Mason's voice had a hardened steel edge, and I could see him as a Marine no problem now.

The resort Security Manager, Ron barreled into the room with a gun strapped on, but it was a stun gun he had out and ready.   He took a position over Ramone since David Bradley wasn't going anywhere or presenting any problem.

Mason looked up. "Did they hurt you?" He asked.

"They didn't have the chance, it happened so fast."

"Hmm, it's a good thing you had that pepper spray with you. That was good thinking." His eyes were mocking.

"Okay, it made a difference. I concede that point." I wasn't going to admit that I'd probably buy stock in the company and never leave home without some in my purse ever again.

Mason wrapped me in his arms for a few moments while the adrenaline started to fade and I began to shake.

"How did you find me? Not that I'm complaining."

"I almost missed it as I was retracing your likely path after work. But, fortunately I saw this just outside the convention center door." He pulled out several crinkled papers from his jacket that were supposed to be inside the file folder I was carrying. "They were scattered along the entry walk. I took a chance and found one of the doors unlocked."

"I've never been so relieved to see you." The words slipped out and I felt me face redden as heat blossomed on my face.

"My words exactly." With that, he nudged my chin and chuckled.

Chapter Twenty-eight

The next few hours were a blur. Detective Lawrence was on the scene quickly and took my statement, even patted me on the back. I figure that's the closest to "sorry" I would ever get.

I called the lawyer, Mr. Chalmers, and he came immediately over to the Convention Center. He presented the information I had gathered, which now might provide the police a jump in understanding about Cynthia and what drove David Bradley and Ramone.

That was a week ago. Mason and Felicia weren't staying at my place anymore. The first night I spent alone I couldn't sleep. I was anxious and had a panic attack. I called Mason and he talked me through. The baby monitors were employed again. Knowing he was on the other end helped. When I did sleep, I had nightmares. My dad flew in and stayed two days until I convinced him to go back home. For those two days of Dad's visit Mason was elusive and they never met...work he said.

I started counseling over Pastor Tom's murder, the break-in, and the attempt on my life. Maybe a little about my mother's death and relationships crept in here and there. It's going well, and I recommend it to any victim of an attack, even a mild one.

The words I had said to David Bradley stuck with me. I did want Pastor Tom's deeds to be revealed, not so much as revenge, but to shed light on the tragic events that hurt many girls. With that in mind, I was meeting with a reporter. John Carlisle wasn't any reporter, and not from the local rag that Tiffany wrote for.

"Ms. LaMere, nice to meet you. I'm Carlisle." We shook hands and we sat.

The coffee shop was a locally owned café downtown and Mr. Carlisle had driven down from Denver branch of the New York Times to discuss the information I had gathered.

"I realize I'm no reporter, and I hadn't verified sources or any of that since I was just trying to round up some alternative suspects for the police. I hope this is of some help in exposing the real Pastor Drake."

"Well, my editor will look over what you've got here and see if we think it's something we want to move forward with. I'd like to ask, why didn't you contact the local paper?"

"They printed an article initially pointing the finger solidly at me, and only me. That has colored my decision on who I should turn this information over to."

I was holding a thumb drive with all of my notes and printouts. "But, there is one thing I ask though." I paused and he nodded to continue.

"There's a lot that is salacious in Pastor Drake's activities that fueled his death. It runs the gamut from cheating on his wife with girls in the church who were likely manipulated; his involvement in a swinger's group that I suspect his wife didn't want to be a part of; a church employee who was misled; his radio ministry partner was impacted by his push for bigger fame; and a leader in the church was blackmailed into silence." I had decided to remove all mention of Peter Patterson. That was between the widow Drake, Peter, and his wife. That truly was nobody else's business.

"Ah, salacious. But not what you wanted? How are you hoping this information will be handled?" He interrupted.

"The other people he impacted have suffered a bit already. I ask you to bear that in mind. There are lessons here. It's a cautionary tale, for youth and parents."

"Hmmm, I imagine the temptation that came with power from his rising position was more than he could resist."

"Avarice, power, control, sex, whatever the vice we're all just human. Perhaps celebrity and faith aren't meant to mix." I said.

I handed him the thumb drive and stood to go. "You can call if you have any questions."

"Perhaps an interview?" His eyebrows perked upward.

"I don't want to be the focus. I shouldn't be the focus. It's the Cynthia and Carmen who need their stories heard." I shook his hand and left feeling I had tried to bring some peace to Cynthia and Carmen...and however many other girls Drake had hurt.

In my car driving back through town traffic, I called Chad on my cell phone.

"Is our new employee ready to get to work?"

"He's eager to get started. He has some great ideas already for harvest hay rides around the resort. I think your idea of a family outing and event coordinator will boost the hotel's family friendly status."

I had contemplated Pastor Drake's blackmail of Crandel, using his need of the job and his being gay to manipulate the situation. One night it came to me that his position as Youth Director had been a rigorous one, with roughly five thousand children of all ages that he kept busy and devised interactive events to educate and entertain, he had the background to get a family events program at the resort off the ground. I sure can learn a lot from him.

That was the big trend in the hospitality industry and we only had one employee to tackle it as an "additional duty". It took some convincing, but Chad got the budget numbers to work after long hours, and he was able to carve out a reasonable salary that would allow him to cover his mother's costs too. I got some training on budgeting throughout the process as well.

I'll never forget his tearful eyes when I handed him the job offer with the salary listed. It made me tear up too. I told him we would be flexible with his schedule so he could spend time with his mother when necessary in the nursing facility where she was suffering from several health issues.

Today was my day off and I didn't want to be late for my first self-defense lesson. That was something I identified in my counseling that would help me feel in control again. Even the basics would be better than my current non-existent skills.

I pulled up to the martial arts studio and parked in one of the empty spots. There weren't any other classmates, I was getting private lessons. I felt a smidgen special.

I hurried to the changing room and got into my typical workout garb, also known as my jogging outfit, of lightweight jogging pants with stripes down the sides and my standard Race for the Cure t-shirt.

I walked into the main area of the dojo where mats covered the floor. I had been briefed beforehand about proper etiquette to use for an official dojo. I bowed upon entering and bowed towards my instructor, who was waiting with arms crossed.

"You're cutting it close. You were nearly late." Mason was all business when it came to martial arts instruction. I would receive no mercy or leniency from him.

"I'll do better sir." Okay, I was hamming it up a bit. But there was a part of me that liked the more formal roles with him. I was still figuring out my feelings. I realized that I could easily be swept off my feet, but I also feared he was only shopping around and wasn't ready to be serious, as evidenced by his absence during dad's visit. I wasn't sure I was ready to be serious for that matter.

I had begun to process through the breakup with Brandon more fully. There was some truth in the accusation that I had been with somebody "safe" and reliable out of fear. Did I really need those qualities, or was it really a security blanket I was clinging to like a child? I still had thinking and soul searching to do before I felt able to consider what could potentially be between Mason and I or how that would look.

"Okay, the first lesson of your self-defense is how to react when being grabbed from behind." His eyes were stormy as he regarded me. *Yep, no mercy in these lessons.* Fortunately, the bruises on my neck from David Bradley had healed.

He proceeded to explain the center of gravity for women was lower than for men. Women's center of gravity is in our hips, whereas men's are in the upper body. If grabbed from behind with an arm around the throat, like what David Bradley had done to me, the first step is to lower the hips like squatting and this causes a male attacker to have to bend over, thus losing an advantage. We practiced and it did make me feel more solid.

The next part was continuing the scenario of an arm around my throat and I practiced securing my breathing so I didn't panic. He instructed me to grab the arm, shrug my shoulders and get my chin down between the arm and my neck to take pressure off, even a little, the windpipe and drop down. That was hard and I wasn't sure about the move, but several practice runs later and I figured adrenaline might also help in an emergency.

Next, he added another move to the sequence. After securing my air way and lowering down a little, I was to focus on the side the arm came from, move the corresponding foot back and behind my attacker's foot so my calf was against the attackers. Once my foot was down, essentially trapping the attacker's leg, I was to pivot my body the direction of my foot so the arm rotated away from my body and broke the hold.

The final step was to then take the attacker's arm and pull it across my body in front, putting the attacker on the floor. I had to use my weight to my advantage. This seemed advanced to me and I was afraid it was too soon. But Mason insisted I keep practicing this move until I wasn't hesitating at each step but moved smoothly from one stage to the next. That took me awhile, but I finally felt like I was getting the hang of it.

"I think that's enough for your first lesson. In the next lessons, you'll learn other approaches from an attacker and how to react. Eventually, I'll mix them up and you will rely on your muscle memory and practice to automatically react according to the given attack mode."

"Sounds like that could take a long time." Despite how much the first lesson had accomplished, this sounded like a long term endeavor and not the quick fix I guess I'd hoped for.

"Well, good self-defense isn't like a scene in a movie. It takes practice and time."

"I don't need to just SING?" I quipped, referring to a popular movie.

"You're asking me to teach you proven methods to defend yourself. That movie advice would be a last resort if you didn't have training. I'm training you in the most effective methods for a variety of attacks."

"Even though this was the first lesson and I'm still getting this move down, I feel better already." I was trying to say thanks.

"I'm glad you asked me to teach you. I was a little surprised, though. Since Brad and Ramone were arrested you've been a little distant." I hadn't realized he felt I was distant.

"We went to Felicia's singing debut." My cousin insisted on singing at Pastor Tom's church even though the killers had been caught. She sang like an angel, but Aunt Regina was upset at me. I was still trying to make it up to her.

"Yes, we both went. But you barely spoke to me."
His voice was low.

"You weren't around when my dad visited. He
wanted to meet you after hearing so much about you."
Aunt Regina and Uncle Lars had made sure my dad
knew about Mason's protection duty. Dad was eager to
scrutinize him. On second thought, maybe it was a
good thing they never met.

"I had a photography job out of town that came up
suddenly. When a friend recommended me to fill in on
a photo shoot for a travel magazine, I jumped at the
chance. It'll help me to build up my freelance
photography business. Ma bichette, is there something
bothering you? Did I do something?"

"A lot has happened for me and I want to make
rational choices." That was vague and non-committal. I
hoped that would suffice without having to explain
further.

The look in his eyes changed and he closed the
distance between us swiftly, confident. One arm snaked
around my waist and pulled me close against him with
his hand against the small of my back. His other hand
held my face in a caress of steel.

"Then you need to make informed decisions. First,
I'm not playing any games here. I'm not a player,
despite what you might think." He said before his lips
made contact.

I have been kissed before, I'm not without some
experience. Perhaps not vast experience like Porsche or

Mason, but I'm not untested. I can honestly say his kiss removed all thought, sent warmth shooting through my body, and had me feeling more alive than any time with Brandon had left me. I felt like I would self-combust in his arms.

I wasn't even aware of my arms encircling his neck or my fingers through his hair until he pulled away. We were both a bit breathless. He rested his forehead against mine.

"Just so you have a frame of reference for your rational decision making. Sometimes you have to take a risk, ma bichette." With that, he released me and walked out of the dojo.

Thank you for reading!

Dear Reader,

I hope you enjoyed ICED: Resort to Murder Mystery #1. I really enjoyed writing the characters of Julienne and Mason and all the neighbors! I hope you enjoyed reading about their adventures, and hope you are looking forward to the next book, NAILED.

Finally, I need to ask you a favor. If you're so inclined, I'd love a review of ICED. Whether you loved it or hated it - I'd just enjoy your feedback. Reviews can be tough to come by these days. You, the reader, have the power now to make or break a book.

Thank you for reading ICED and spending time with me.

In gratitude,
Avery Daniels

ABOUT THE AUTHOR

Avery Daniels was born and raised in Colorado, graduated from college with a degree in business administration, and has worked in fortune 500 companies and Department of Defense her entire life. Her most eventful job was apartment management for 352 units. She still resides in Colorado with two brother black cats as her spirited companions. She volunteers for a cat shelter, enjoys scrapbooking and card making, photography, and painting in watercolor and acrylic. She inherited a love for reading from her mother and grandmother and grew up talking about books at the dinner table.

Website: www.Avery-Daniels.com
Signup for my newsletter:
facebook.com/AveryDanielsAuthor

Next in Resort to Murder Mysteries is Nailed